A FOOLPROOF PLAN

Books by D.D. Cross

A Foolproof Plan
The Flesh Mechanics
Timeclot
Timeclot II: Stroke of Genes
Chrome Plated Corns
Me and Mr. Mephistopheles
Onions Bunions Corns and Dungeons
A Den of Brigands
Field of Corns
Forheavenstake
Back to Hades: Eustice Seeney Returns to Hell
Go to Hell! (I DID): Interview with Eustice Seeney
Devilzinthedetails
Hellitainteasy
Heapatrouble

A FOOLPROOF PLAN

D.D. CROSS

A Foolproof Plan is a work of fiction. Names, characters, places, and incidents are the products of the author's imagination or are used fictitiously. Any resemblance to actual events, locales, or persons, living or dead, is entirely coincidental. While the hotel mentioned is a real establishment, its portrayal is fictionalized.

Original Art by D.D. Cross

Published by the MMA Publishing Group International

ISBN: 979-8-218-92517-8

Manufactured in the United States of America

If it sounds too good to be true it most certainly is.

THE STASH

Hidden within a canyon along the continental slope of the 25,000 foot deep Cayman Trench, also known as the Bartlett Deep, between Jamaica and the tip of Cuba lies a retrofitted WWII Type XXI U-boat, a storage site. The recently modified U-boat's hull is reinforced to withstand depths exceeding its location at four hundred feet. An anechoic coating cloaks its exterior, blending with the surrounding volcanic rock formations and deep-water coral. Strategically placed it's close enough yet not too far from shipping lanes, hidden from prying eyes. The U-boat operates with whispering electric motors, making detection beneath the thermocline layer nearly impossible. However, recent seismic events jeopardize the submerged vessel, and for a den of brigands time is running out.

1

PARADOX PARADISE

The Cayman Islands are a British Territory nestled in the Western Caribbean. There are three islands: Grand Cayman, Cayman Brac, and Little Cayman, known for stunning seas, vibrant marine life, diving, snorkeling, fishing, dining, white sand beaches, and the benefits of international banking. The widely known magical serenity is avoidance of prying eyes, and Grand Cayman, the largest of the three and perpetually developing, is where banks outnumber beach goers, and money could quietly rest. When global laws and treaties began making shadowy funds exposed to investigatory light, a certain chaos shifted the mood on the island. It became less than comfortable for funds derived from nefarious dealings. However, properly cleansed funds could remain beneath a beach umbrella, and those were becoming scarce.

Thomas Kurfew sat at the beachfront open-air bar, and drummed his fingers on the Lucite counter embedded with gold doubloons. He figured they were as phony as the bartender's buoyant jabbering with day-drinkers. It was dark beneath the tin roof of Romeo Roy's Rodeo Tiki Bar and Grill. He stared at the boats off shore nearing the horizon, and shook his head listening to the arrhythmic tick of a rickety ceiling fan. Time tiptoed by with each murmur of reggae stuttering out of an aging jukebox. His head ached with each beat of the kettle drum. Time was running out. The bartender was leaning toward a goatee'd man in a white sports coat and straw fedora hat. Sipping a beer two stools to his right was a tank topped woman in a baseball cap. They shot a glance in what seemed to be a mind your own business gaze, and carried on with their conversation. Behind him, two suited men sat in a booth sipping their drinks, and spoke in what he imagined was some shared hidden knowledge. The sort he'd had enough of, and went back to his empty shot-glass next to another, and the plastic ashtray smoldering with semi-crushed butts.

“Hit me again.” Thomas held up his glass.

The bartender pushed himself with both hands from the counter, held up a wait a minute finger at the couple, righted himself, tossed a bar rag over his shoulder, and brushed dreadlocks from his face. Fugazi as the coins in the counter, like everything else he’d seen since Catherine left.

“Ready for another good buddy?” The bartender shook his head and smiled. His teeth were huge, Thomas would later recall, and looked like dice cubes on a white felt poker table.

“Make it a double cowboy.”

“Y’all drinkin’ yer good ole self stupid?”

Kurfew stared at the second hand oozing across the face of his wristwatch. A gold on gold Rolex Submariner.

“Snap out’ve it buckaroo.”

“Why?”

“High time you settle up the tab.”

“You’ve got a charge card on file, use it.”

“Izzat fine watch the real deal?

Romeo put put his lips together and frowned. “Uh uh, that Black Amex charge card, unlimited credit. Hoo-wee boy, it’s done been cancelled, or maybe that lady may’ve done some tinkerin’ fouled it up.‘ “Broads do that ya know. Maybe she reported it stole.”

Thomas stared at the man and shut his eyes.“Maybe some day I’ll find out. About that drink?”

“You’ve been here every mornin’ since she upped and split. Um hmm, she was a right fine filly Tommy. You scare her off, or run out of dough? Maybe the old whiskey dick drove her off the ranch. Sometimes ya never know what's real when it comes to women."

"Don't call me Tommy, and what do you know about what's real, and even if reality isn't just an illusion?"

"Don't go gettin' metaphysical on me." Romeo inhaled and blew out the words slowly, "See that yacht over yonder, that's real, this bar, real, about the tab and that watch, them's real."

"About that drink."

"You're lucky Tommy," Romeo stared at the timepiece, "we can settle up right now, do us some horse tradin'."

Kurfew undid the clasp, slid the watch off, and handed it to Romeo. "How much?"

"I'd have to appraise it." Romeo held it up, weighed it in his palm, and ran some water over it at the bar's sink, and said, "Tommy, that hummin' second hand, weight, and gettin wet, says I'll give y'all a dime for it."

"Three dimes and we're good Romeo."

"Three dimes huh?" Romeo Roy stepped back and scratched his chin. "Lemme go check somethin'," and disappeared into a room at the back of the bar.

Kurfew gazed at the squeaky ceiling fan, counted the rotations and waited. He figured Romeo might swap it for a fake, or lowball the price. When he reappeared he wore a white Stetson hat. The wig was gone, one eye narrowed, and a grin that meant business. He slid a manilla envelope across the counter with the name Thomas Kurfew, MD beneath his manicured fingertips. "Here's twenty-five thou, US good buddy. That ought make us even." He stepped back and put his hands on his hips. "You gonna open it?"

Kurfew stared at the envelope and said nothing.

"Go on, check it out. You've been livin' like a rat Kurfew. Crashin' wherever ya'll could. That fine place ya'll shared with your lady is in the process of bein' dee-molished. That there's progress. "What's your deal cowboy, drink yer self dead? Dyin' ain't much of a livin' son."

"Any idea where she's gone?" Kurfew watched the bartender smile, adjust his bolo tie, and waited for the bullshit.

Romeo Roy spread his arms, shook his head, and shrugged. "Hell no, ain't my problem. Don't spend that dough all in one place. Unless it's here good buddy."

"I'll take that as a positive affirmation."

Romeo turned to the bar well paused for a beat, and grabbed a bottle of Glenlivet from the top shelf. "This is you're lucky day," he set the bottle over a huge doubloon, shoved aside the ashtray, bent toward Thomas, and whispered, "You got some folks been pokin' `round askin' questions."

“About me? Isn’t that special. Who else do I owe money to?”

“They was serious types Tommy.”

“So, I’m a professional drunkard that got ditched by his gal without even a fuck off kiss. What were they asking?”

“Some bull pucky `bout your missing lady, and your high falutin ways.”

Kurfew showed no expression knowing it would unsettle Romeo’s rant. “And what’d you have to say?”

“Ain’t no snitch. I don’t know but for nothin’ down here. Y’all know that bartender customer confidentiality thing what with you bein’ a doctor and all.”

“Is that how it is Romeo?”

"Sort've an honor among thieves thing Huh?"

"Yeah, good buddy. The way I think somebody's wantin' to have a sit down with you, and that somebody had John Q Law writ on em. And I gotta say they meant business, and not the kind I'd take light. Shee-yatt I'd be on the move iffen those sorts had some Q and A for me. Thass why I blew `em off."

"What'd you do?"

"I oft put on my full country bumpkin in paradise voice, and dummy up when folks go pokin' `round. Especially if they seem outta place. I give em the 'I don't know but for nothin' not a thing' routine. Shuts em up right quick."

"I'm goin' to check into a decent hotel, and get some things in order."

"I reckon that's gonna be a long stay good buddy. Maybe dry out, clean up, and skedaddle on back to the U.S. of A." Romeo tipped his hat.

"Maybe, maybe not. The bitch took my passport."

"No passport Tommy. Shee-yatt that filly done took ya ziff you was a rodeo clown, son. She's nothin' but trouble. Oh yeah, I forgot, last time I saw her she left a goodbye letter."

"You didn't mention that Romeo."

"Easy boy, it was one of those dear asshole letters. Figured you'd end up with a bum liver, and I hate losin' a good customer. I read it, course I read it. Some bull-pucky broads write when they give ya the blow off. You want it?"

Kurfew narrowed his eyebrows, pointed his right index finger at the bartender. "You saved it?"

"Shit yeah. It's in with that money, a busted phone I couldn't get workin', and a lottery ticket she done wrote on. It was a dud."

“Or maybe it fell outta her bag right cowboy?”

“Yup, plum fell on out with some pills too. Capsules three, four, somethin’ like that. I put `em in the package, don’t want no dope here, thass why I put your doctor’s name on there.”

“How considerate of you Romeo. Yeah, right.”

“Y’all ain’t gonna count the cash, check out the goodies in there, cry over the bye bye letter, and get hammered?”

“Not today. I trust you Romeo. Stiffin’ customers isn’t good for business. Besides I know where to find you if you did. Enjoy the watch.”

“Yes you do Tommy, right here. Romeo shot a glance at his new wristwatch, held it up to his ear and nodded. “A fine timepiece. I like it.”

“I’m out’ve here Romeo.” Kurfew grinned inwardly. He had this prick just where he wanted. He stood casually as if he was another addled boozer, yet absorbing faces and body language. Assets or threats, registering the layout of the bar, and stepped out into the sun. He walked three minutes to his right, turned, and doubled back. Three Asian men passed him on their way into the saloon as if he was a hologram, and their hair was perfect. Ahead, no tail, not yet.

Seven minutes and thirty seconds after Thomas Kurfew left the bar, Romeo whispered to the man in the fedora. His name was Harold Spooky Pollack. "You're here Spooky to work off a debt. Now get with the program, or you're gonna owe me a whole lot more. Go on git a move on with the crew, and don't foul things up." He notched his chin at the men in the booth. "You boys ready? Ain't no time for lollygaggin, I gotta find out what Kurfew's up to, and meet some Chinks."

2

KURFEW

With some cash on hand he could sort things out, get back into shape, and maybe finagle a few miles out of the Amex card with a few phone calls. Anything to get off the island.

Two weeks, two days, three hours, and twenty minutes after checking into the Grand Island Luxury Hotel which in Kurfew's estimation was a dump. He studied his reflection in the bathroom mirror. Sober, the shakes and tremors gone. Showered, strong, clear-headed, shaved, and tanned enough to pass as a tourist. He ignored the stray, untrimmed hair, and wandered into the room, dressed, and stared at the contents on the bed. He examined the phone, cords, chargers, and the rest of the items, and saw pieces of a puzzle that didn't come together.

Four capsules which no pharmacy could identify, the goodbye letter, and the lottery ticket. What the fuck are these, he asked himself, suicide pills? Shit, not today. He cracked open one of the pills, stared at the yellow powder and poured it into the glass of water on the nightstand. He then swirled it around, and waited. Finally he arranged the goodbye note and lottery ticket on the bed, and poured, one drop at a time, then a dollop on the papers. Nothing. He cracked open the other capsules, mixed them with warm water and saturated the notes. The unseen became visible. It was a message: "61J, SERE, survive, evade, resist, escape." An escape code he knew from his army days that didn't make sense. Numbers and letters. He had to step away. What is this shit? He put the do not disturb sign on the door and went for a walk.

After a coffee and an egg, and two hours wandering, something struck. They were instructions. A warning, maybe a threat. 61J, his MOS, combat surgeon. It wasn't just a simple cipher on how to activate the phone. It was a command.

In the suite, Kurfew went to work on the device, removing the SIM card, rinsing it in the cocktail, and punching in some numbers. Beneath the written scrawl the lottery ticket's numbers matched a bank account, no, not enough digits. A phone number? Shit, now what? He stared and waited, finally dozing off.

At 4AM the phone vibrated, a text message appeared on the screen, a series of digits, latitude and longitude. He stared at the message for ten minutes and the mini-bar for twenty.

"Shit, now what?" He said aloud. Stood, stretched, showered, and got dressed. He packed, counted out what remained of the twenty-five thousand, and stopped himself from calling the concierge when he heard a series of metallic taps on the door, waited a beat and heard it again louder. Fuck whoever it was had a gun. Evade and fucking escape. No time to fuss. He made his exit by window, ran onto the terrace, and walked slowly toward the main drag avoiding anyone or anything at the hotel, parking lot, especially CCTVs.

He walked a half mile before hailing the first cab that came along. It was the only taxi and seemed to Kurfew a bit odd, almost contrived. He sized up the rickety Mercedes Diesel's driver, not a threat, and if he was wrong it wouldn't take much to neutralize him. "Take me to Romeo Roy's Tiki Bar, chop-chop."

It was a five-minute ride, but the bar wasn't.

Ten minutes of wondering what the fuck was going on. No one around, everyone a stranger. "Cabby, get me to the airport fast," Kurfew paused a beat, no passport, shit. "The docks. Take me to the harbor."

"By the way," the taxi driver said, "My name is Calvin, and fast is going to cost you an extra twenty dollars. I don't want no trouble speeding, mon. What's de hurry?"

"Any chance you know anything about the Tiki bar being gone?"

"Some say a fire, some say de demolition. Been shut for a week. De owner he's no good. Some police and men in suits been lookin' for de owner. He's gone. They lookin' for de guy. Big trouble."

"Romeo's on the run?"

"You know him? There's a reward if they catch him. He had a big boat, a yacht, too big and not welcome, use up too much fuel. He's gone, been couple weeks now, mon."

"Take me to the harbor where Romeo fueled his boat. You do know where that's at, right?"

"Everyone knows where dat is, mon."

"Is that a problem?"

"I can drive you to the docks but," he looked at the passenger in the rearview, "Police and who knows who's be snoopin' `round. What happens there ain't on me."

"Drive cabby. You show up on a deserted road out-of-nowhere for a fare, what's that shit?"

"Coincidence, big competition, de money's good dis time a day. Any cops we get there, ain't sayin' nothin'."

"Fine." Kurfew put his suspicion on hold.

"Why you gotta go there, troubles wit de law or maybe you got some kind of funny business?"

"I want a boat, good money you hook me up."

"Hook you up, um hmm, cash money."

"Five hundred USD for you, more for someone who's no regular at Cowboy Romeo's late dump, and wants to make some cash." The driver said nothing. They rode in silence beneath a reddened predawn light. A warm breeze blew through the open windows.

The cab stopped beside a shanty. Near enough to the docks so Thomas could hear the waves slapping against hulls, and masts rise and fall. The air was pleasantly warm. He felt some tension being relieved as the reddish dawn sky began to turn to a deep hue of blue. They were far enough from the road. Two phones hung on the side of the hut. It was an abandoned dry goods and fueling depot that had seen better days. The upscale station nearby was bustling with coffee sipping gamefish snobs, decked out in high end threads, chatting away in loud, yet inaudible tones about their nautical adventures, or next big score. Who knows, it was Grand Cayman and anything that goes, went, was spent, saved, hidden, or withdrawn.

Kurfew placed a call to the number on the lottery ticket. It went to voicemail. He didn't leave a message. Ten minutes later Calvin was counting the money, shaking his head.

“What’s next Calvin?”

“There’s a sailor, she’s good, she’s smart, and she can handle herself. And she ain’t got no good reason to turn down good money.”

“How long until she—”

“She what?”

“She’s comin’ to meet us.”

“She have a name?”

“Yes, mon.”

Before Kurfew got an answer a woman’s voice said, “You a cop or something?”

“No, I lean toward avoiding those types.”

“You look like some kinda law or some kinda runnin’ away sort.”

"She's Canadian, a good friend of my family." Calvin stepped back. "And she's no friend of dat Romeo or the police."

"Why's that?" Kurfew gazed at the woman, maybe he thought longer than he should.

She wore a dark bandana with strands of hair dancing in the light breeze. Her tan was deep, and she had a spray of freckles across her nose, sculpted cheek bones, sunglasses, and stood a good four inches shorter than his six feet. She had a Grateful Dead T-shirt over small firm breasts, cutoff jeans, and deck shoes. There was something about her he couldn't put his finger on, and maybe, he thought it'd be something to not think too hard about.

The woman pointed her chin at the cab driver. "Shoo Calvin, I can handle this," she faced Kurfew and in deep husky words, "What're you staring at hotshot?"

"You lady. I've seen you somewhere. I can't place where."

"Oh please, spare the charm fella. I don't need this shite before lunch."

Thomas watched her remove a pack of cigarettes, extract one slowly, tap it on the pack, and place it between her lips. She studied Kurfew's face, shoes, height, and posture. She lit her cigarette with a disposable lighter, inhaled, and lowered her shades. "You don't look like a narc. More of a guy on the run. What're you carryin', dope, money, some other go-to-jail lagniappes?"

"I didn't get your name."

"I didn't give it. Keeps creeps guessing." She exhaled blowing out a plume of smoke and smiled. "Calvin said you wanted off the island. Starting price ten K US. Ya got it stud?"

"How far does ten K go lady?"

"Not far enough. You look knackered. On the run, aren't ya. Got some barney, huh?"

"What's with the accent lady?"

"What's it your business?"

"The not into getting fucked business."

"Yeah, heard about you, Thomas Kurfew. Getting the blow off from the gal you were with."

"It was business."

"The sort where she does a Houdini with a nice stash, and leaves you with shit business?"

"The not any of your whatever your name is business. What should I call you, Sea Witch?"

"Cute, big guy. You can call me Meredith. You're on the run, probably have more cash iced away, and want off the island. Right?"

"I was hoping for a pleasure cruise."

"A comedian." She tossed her head back and laughed. It was a strained laugh punctuated by a cough. A shock of hair tumbled down to her shoulders, she took a drag from her cigarette and stared at him.

"What're you lookin' at?"

Something about her, the cut of her face, that something foreign yet domestic, Kurfew felt drawn to. "Are you up for this Meredith?"

"Cheeky bugger, aren't we?" Her eyes widened as she blew out a plume of smoke that matched her gray-green eyes. "Where are you hoping to go hotshot?"

"I need to get to the US."

"Maybe you ought to drop your need a few notches big guy." She took another drag, inhaled deep, and turned sideways. "Calvin mentioned some issues with Romeo, eh?"

The cab driver hadn't left and chimed in, "I told her you was a regular customer for de last month at Romeo Roy's Bar."

Meredith shot Calvin a side glance. “I thought you were leaving.”

“Calvin,” Thomas stared into his eyes, waited a beat. “What’re you my tail? Did your cab show up out of nowhere?”

“No, no, nothin’ like dat, mon. It’s a small island. Everyone that takes care of the high rollin’ money people talks, and knows every ting mon that goes on here.”

“Oh, that makes sense in that screw you bullshit way. I suppose you have an in with everyone here, from the bankers, boozers, dopers, hookers, and money washers, huh?”

Thomas had an edge on he couldn’t shake. Maybe it was the broad he said to himself. It’d been a while.

Calvin shrugged, and Ms. bandana shook her head, smirked, and locked eyes with Kurfew. “If he’s not a muppet and sober enough to not barf on my boat he'd realize no way no how a sailboat's going to the States. Too far." Meredith flicked her cigarette into the water. "You need a plane, and these days you're gonna need a pro that can dodge not only the Cubans, but the stinking US Coast Guard."

"Commercial flights don't take cash, and I'm not using a charge card."

Kurfew's phone vibrated, another message. "I've gotta see who this is."

"I can't be arsed with phone shit." She started to walk away. If you hurry the cabby might be nearby."

"Cool it lady," Kurfew held up his index finger, "Hang on."

The message, a series of letters and numbers. Latitude and longitude? Stat, $ 4 U. Fat. Your Esq.

“Who was that tan man? Your parole officer? The long arm of the law, or your dope connection?”

“If you can get me to these coordinates,” he held up the phone, “There’s serious bank in it.”

“What’s serious?” Bandana reached for another cigarette.

“What’s with the cute, rhyming, slang, business lady?”

“It’s a mystery innit?” She shook her head.

Two gunshots sent a flock of birds skyward, and a hush fell over the harbor. Kurfew lept in front of Jerry Garcia and shoved her to the ground brushing a hand over her breasts, crouched and moved toward the shanty, poking his head around the side. Calvin was on the ground, two men in dark suits rummaging through the cabby’s clothes. They stood, side to side scanning the area, then in slow, deliberate movements moved toward the wharf, hand signaling each other, and pausing briefly every few steps and vectoring in on Kurfew and the woman.

"Git yer hands off my tits?" Chin pointed to the boats. "I'm outta here, you comin' asshole?"

"Which boat is yours? I can't hold these guys off," running.

"None."

"The fuck you mean, none?" Kurfew had eyes on the men. Is this a ruse by a pathetic dock-rat, or a setup when another shot was fired. Move. Fuckit at least the chick didn't have a gun between her tits.

The men in suits were at the shanty, one in front of the other facing the road, both making side-to-side twitches sizing up any onlookers, calculating their vantage point. These were pros, Kurfew thought, and he was either in the getting dead zone, or she was.

"What the fuck is none?"

“Not now, just follow me. It’s not my boat follow me or we’re both screwed.”

“Shit, I hope you know what you’re doing Sea Witch.”

“The Cigarette boat moored at the end of dock, that’s the one. There’s a gun in the cooler grab it. You know how to use it don’t you?”

Kurfew opened the cooler. It was a Heckler & Koch VP9 Tactical OR. The choice of military, law enforcement, and security organizations around the world. The fuck is with this broad. What the fuck’s with me. I don’t want to remember why I know this shit. The engines kicked up and the boat tore away from the wharf ripping the tow lines and cleats. Bitch can drive this thing. Kurfew fired off a few rounds hitting a fuel pump. An explosion, flames and a dark feather of smoke tickled the sky.

At top speed the speedboat’s wake made the boat a blip on the horizon.

"Throttle back lady, we're clear of those jokers. We're in open seas, and you're bleeding." Kurfew saw blood on her left leg, put down the gun, and took a closer look, "Gotta get that wound cleaned up. Is there a first aide kit on board?"

"In the cabin. What're you gonna do patch me up?"

"No, I'm gonna slip on the blood and break my wrist. C'mon, stop with the assholery, I'm stuck with you, and don't need the headache of an infection." His voice deep, loud, and audible, over the idling engines. She stared at him as if she'd register the words as tender, maybe caring. Kurfew knew that and watched her swivel in the pilot's seat, stand, and take his hand.

She narrowed her eyes, raised the corner of her mouth north. "What about the boat?"

"We're far enough out, it'll drift. Current's not strong enough to do much."

“Then what?” She ducked her head as they climbed three steps into the dark cabin. “Shut down the bloody engines.”

3

An hour, maybe two later the sound of thunder echoed. It wasn't engines, no fuel. Kurfew'd fallen asleep below, and focused into a fuzzy consciousness. He poked his head out of the cabin. He saw a pinpoint in the cloudless sky. It wasn't thunder, a plane engine droned.

Kurfew shaded his eyes as if saluting with both hands, adjusting to the midday light. He watched the plane circle, drop altitude, and approach. It was a yellow vintage craft with pontoons. Far away and much too close, "Meredith, snap out of it, we've got company, a seaplane."

No answer, he climbed back into the cabin where the woman was dozing. A syringe next to her. Her leg elevated, blood spots on the dressing. She'd live, he thought. The wound pierced muscle and tendon, sparing the major blood vessels and nerves. A makeshift procedure using fish hooks, fine lines, and pliers. Suitable instruments, yet he considered would make for some pain. The refrigerator in the galley stocked with beer, water, stale food, and cereal. There were shelves and drawers, a ship-to-shore phone, an ancient CB radio setup, and a pair of high end, to his thinking, computers. Whose fucking boat was this? He began ripping through whatever wherever and found a first aide kit, antibiotic cream, bandages, syringes, and a vial of morphine. That'd do. He went to work, starting with the morphine, she resisted at first, but finally got woozy and compliant. He rinsed the wound, did the repair, tied the last suture, put together a field dressing, and lay beside her and dozed. He awoke to the sounds up top. He moved her head from his shoulder, sat back next to the woman, checked her vitals, and nudged her. In her semi-stuporous state she muttered something about her phone, where was it. Nowhere he could find and wasn't going to pat her down. There was a note in her hand, Thomas figured she'd gotten when he nodded out. On it was a call signal. The name Larry

Kaminsky Esq, was scrawled on it with numbers. Larry, the piece of shit disbarred attorney, go-between, half criminal, government informant, schmuck, who'd gotten him set up with the mess he'd left on Grand Cayman.

"Meredith, wake up," he squeezed her upper arms gently. "Do you know Larry?"

"The chubby guy," slurring. "Larry's comin' for us." And without ceremony proceeded into a wheeze, a gasp, and slipped deeply into a stupor.

***

The yellow single engine seaplane landed with a series of uneasy splashes, thumping on rivulets of a stirred up sea. Sputtered and came to an idle within swimming distance of the speedboat. Thomas watched the craft float toward them, the propeller fanning the stillness of the midday breeze.

"Ahoy motherfuckers!"

The shouting man wore a straw hat over a huge, round head, and too-tight tropical shirt. He used both hands to pull himself out of the ancient plane, stood on a pontoon, and lowered his sunglasses. “Kurfew what took you so long?” Chubby shouted to the pilot, a silver haired black man. “Chalk, get these rummies on board. We’re only a few yards away, we’ll drift right to em.”

“This is a rescue Larry? Shit.”

“Thomas, I knew you needed off the island.”

“Why you Larry, you got me into this mess?”

“You needed saving buddy, I’m your guy.”

“Yeah, sure you are shitbird. You set me up.”

“You agreed to the deal, and fucked up.” The chubby man shook his head.

“Now you can make things right Kurfew.”

“How’s that Larry?”

“We’ll go over it when we’re outta here.”

“Wounded on board, is there space Larry?”

“If it’s fine with the pilot, sure bring her.”

“How’d you know it was a her Larry?”

“Just get a move on, we gotta ditch the boat.”

Thomas spread his arms at the open water and stared at the fat man, “I never trusted you shit-bird, but for now I’ll make an exception. He was easing Meredith onto the plane, an arm around her waist. The pilot was standing on a pontoon, rear hatch open, taking the woman’s arm and arranging the seat. “Plenty of space,” he nodded at Kurfew, and shot a glance at Larry that if looks killed Larry’d be on life support. “She’ll be just fine.”

“Thanks Chalk.”

“I believe we’re in for some stormy weather.”

The pilot stepped back into the cockpit.

"When you hear me out, you'll thank me."

Thomas put his hands on his hips "I doubt it Larry. You need me for something and that something's got favor bank written all over it."

"Other way around buddy. You need me."

Kurfew watched the pilot maneuvering the port window. He wore aviator sunglasses and nodded before lazily dropping his left arm out the hatch. Thomas's gaze fixed on the faded tattoo and grinned inwardly, raised his hand, began to salute, paused, and brushed his hand across his hair.

***

The flight plan was simple Larry explained, "We're gonna land in Miami, sort of on the out-skirts, and you and me are flying commercial to Big Town, where you'll pay a visit to a chap who'll lead us to another chap, and whatever went missing from the Grand Cayman stash with your former lady will be recovered. That simple."

"Nothing's simple with you. What's the plan?"

"You scope out a guy's operation, shake him down and see what falls out.

"Who's the guy, a dope dealing, art pimp?"

"Frontman for big money crime bosses."

"What about Meredith, Larry?"

"She's disposable, gets cut loose in Miami. When we land she goes her way, capice?

"I'm not ditching her. I've done enough shitty things and no way I'm adding abandoning her. Get it Larry?"

"Oh, Dr. Righteous nowadays, huh? Three ex-wives, big shot surgeon, ex-major runnin' with the mercs on oh so secret missions. Fuck you and your newfound conscience Thomas."

"I'll snap your chubby neck Larry if you don't come clean with me." Kurfew had his right arm across Larry's neck and started to squeeze. "Who is this frontman, another one of your shit-bird connections?"

"You're choking me man! He's some foreign putz in the slums of Big Town. I'll make the arrangements, set you up in a pad, and we'll be good to go."

"And Catherine?" Kurfew released the chokehold, leaned back, and adjusted his seat-belt.

"Screw her. She screwed you over, fucked Uncle Sam, and a dozen mobbed up scumbags. Don't worry about the bitch. Wah wah, she broke your heart, get over it. "She's not gonna give a shit if you turn up dead. Don't go pokin' around tryin' ta find that bitch."

"What've I got to lose Larry?"

"Aside from your life?"

"I've heard that kind of bullshit from you in the past Larry."

"Think of it this way Thomas, what do you have to lose?" Larry softened his tone. "Listen brother, if things go right you'll be set. I need you to get in there, and do what needs to be done. You'll be helping out yourself and doin' me a solid. There's no other way to get back what you lost. You do this Thomas, decorated soldier, combat surgeon, you get the world by the balls again, the shit you want. All you've gotta do is follow the plan."

"As in reinstating my medical license, a quiet practice, nice place to live, and far away from my ex-wives." Thomas figured he'd toss Larry the know-it-all disaster master what I want dipshit, a misdirect. First things first finding the right puzzle for the mutating pieces. Things were fluid, and none of it was any of shitbird's business. Not yet.

"There'll be a nice cut of what we recover Thomas, I can promise you that."

"Sure there is, promises promises Larry."

Meredith stirred, opened her eyes and mumbled, "Anyone have a cigarette?" She lowered her baseball cap'a brim, tucked her chin, and gave coughed softly.

"No." Larry turned to face her and shouted "Go back to sleep sugar, we'll be in Miami soon."

"Ain't yer sugar, fat man." She muttered.

"Don't get your panties in a bind bee-yatch."

"She's wounded Larry, gotta get her some antibiotics, check out that leg. Gimme your phone, I know where to take her when we land, and I need some down time before whatever you've got planned." Thomas shoved his hand at Larry.

"Hand over your phone." Waited a beat, "Larry why'd she have your contact, was she with you on some other bent deal?"

"She's does bit work here and there. Make your dipshit call. Don't use up my battery."

"Would you keep it down, fellas," Meredith mumbled, "I've got me some mates to see in Miami."

Thomas noticed the bandana was swapped, and through some haze recalled recognizing the baseball cap through a drunken blur he couldn't place, and filed it under the things to consider part of his mind. "Affairs can wait Meredith. Shit, I'll have one of my guys, a plastic surgeon meet you at Miami International first, he's an old friend and owes me. Is that okay with you Larry?"

"If that'll make you happy T, how about you honey?"

"I'm not your honey fat boy. Listen love, I'm bloody good on my own." Meredith raised her voice a few octaves before shutting her eyes.

"She's out of it Thomas, you wanna be a boy-scout, fine. The broad, forget about her. Far as I know she's a doper. The last thing you need, and don't think I didn't catch the way you cozied up to her. Cut her loose and don't get lost we've got to be in Big Town, time's runnin' out before the shit hits and crap splatters."

"You've got it all figured out Larry" Chalk murmured in a tone reserved for an upright bass riff, paused, and unceremoniously plucked away. "A regular foolproof plan."

"The fuck Chalk, just fly the plane. I'll make it worth your while. Then go have a beer, maybe a few."

Kurfew leaned forward, "You're pretty edgy Larry. I know there's shit you're not mentioning, but if I do get fucked on this caper, or whatever it is, you'll be wishing being a fat man without balls was your only problem."

"Relax Thomas, I've got enough pressure on me. When we land there's a duffle stowed away with cash, a credit card, and a burn phone, answer it when it rings. Go unwind in Miami for a few day's. Get some new threads, and put yourself together."

The plane banked hard, engine revved, and dove to a lower altitude. The pilot's voice switched to a seasoned pro. Spoke in a calm, even, taciturn tone of airline pilots heading for stormy weather. "Tighten your seat-belts, we're approaching a heavily surveilled airspace. We may do some tight maneuvering. We might have to ditch this thing, so be ready. If y'all got anything to say to each other do it now."

"One more thing Thomas." Larry turned to face Kurfew.

"Final words of bullshit Larry?"

“Ain’t no bullshit buddy. You’re wanted for questioning about the missing Catherine and they’ve got you, Thomas, pegged for the missing stash.”

“I don’t know where she is Larry, and if I knew where the stash was I sure’s shit wouldn’t be here with you would I?”

“No, that’d make for one sucker’s move.”

“Who’s the they Larry?”

“It’s a long list Thomas.”

The plane’s cabin pressure shifted with the rapid descent. Pontoons bounced once, twice, three times, before leveling off a few yards above the calm waters off the coast of Southeast Florida. The owner of the two hundred sixty foot yacht with a stealth gray hull and angular profile was awaiting their arrival. He watched with Steiner Military M1050R 10x50 LRF binoculars, and smiled. “It’s about time. Collsarn pilot got no brains usin’ that ole smuggler’s move, ain’t been used since the last century. Dumbass." He wore a white Stetson hat, and what several of the ship's twenty crew members would describe as huge dice cube teeth.

A FEW DAYS LATER: BIG TOWN USA

4

It was the sort of neighborhood where bad habits grew like a colony of mutant rats that nibbled on the residents fingers and toes. The air was thick from misery, cheap wine, desperation, and the Dumpsters brimmed with rotting nothingness and forgotten dreams.

This was the center of Big Town. The remains of what used to be a thriving community. Along the boulevard were going out-of-business mom-and-pop shops, shot and a beer day drinker havens, a dentist's shingle sagged above a dirty window. Next door was a bail bondsman, then a laundromat, and a massage parlor. Squeezed between was a general practitioner's office. On its window were the letters with a phrase from another generation, "Welcome Walk-Ins."

Streetwalkers fondled their cigarettes and exhaled a “Hey mister,” to any passing vehicle. There weren’t many, and their doors were locked.

I asked myself is this the right address? Is this where the doctor parks his Bentley? It was. The vanity license tag gave it away. And the woman washing it was Dr. Zillonious Crum's bimmy who gave me a scowl the way an antibiotic does at bacteria.

Crum, word on the street, was an expert in all things unwholesome, and then some. He was the go-to guy in the “special medication” and insurance scam racket, and had a rep for taking book, fencing stolen goods, putting money on the street, and washing more cash than the laundromat next door washed soiled undies.

I was going to be a Walk-In this morning.
I opened the door to Crum’s office and took it in. A sense of a bad hangover washed over me. What have I stepped into?

The waiting room decor was of the sort favored by the Salvation Army, or a repurposed army barracks, and had a cloyingly sweet smell. There were crumpled 1970s National Geographic and Time magazines scattered on the thrift store coffee table, and the dark walls had photos of Zill and some third rate porn stars gone legit. They still had that used up pout broads in the skin flicks use to entice. They were far from pretty. Either was the dame behind the pebble glass, who saw me hovering around the waiting room to see the great Doc. Her name tag said Dixie, and by her accent she wasn't doing much whistling. Her lipstick was smudged, and the top two buttons of her blouse were undone, revealing a tight bra containing a pair of Zeppelin's ready to float up to the ceiling fan.

"Can I help you?" She bit down on her lower lip and ran her tongue along it fast, as she leaned back. “Do you have an appointment?” She said it with a gasp of gin soaked fumes that made my eyes water.

“Do I need one? There's no one here Dixie?”

“You have to fill out some forms,” she said in a tone reserved for traffic cops, tollbooth operators, and dogcatchers.

“It’s personal Dixie, I’m not a patient.”

“You’ve got a name bubby?”

“Yes, I do and you don’t need it.”

“Is it secret?”

“I’m a doctor. A secret one.”

“Smart aleck, huh?”

“Pretty much.”

She turned and spoke over her shoulder a few decibels under a shout, “Docta Crum there’s a guy out here says he’s got somethin’ personal for ya. Says he’s a docta.”

The door to the waiting room opened and a huge, hard coughing, Cossack spoke, "Hey you, come in." That was the first time I met Zillonious Crum.

It should have been the last.

5

CRUM

He was a huge man with pale skin and white hair sprouting out as if he'd been shocked by a few thousand volts. The mustache was salt and pepper and matched his enormous eyebrows that raised with every shift of his yellow tinged eyes, and looked like caterpillars screwing in some frantic terrarium style. He wore a white suit with a bloody red shirt that matched his tie. Both hung over his bloated gut stained with who knows what.

"What is bringing you to the office today no Meester doctor no name. " The caterpillar brows went to humping. "You are maybe police, or don't want to be seen in this part of town, no?"

"Figured I'd do some slumming."

"You say this is slum wise guy. What are you doing here?"

"I've got a message for you Crum. A warning."

Crum tossed his head back and laughed mirthlessly. "A warning? Ha. Nobody warns the Zill. Do you know who I am beeg shot?"

"Did you forget?"

Crum leaned forward. "Nobody threatens the Zill, You not hear me?" His face reddened.

"I do. Listen, this wasn't my top choice of things to do this morning."

"Maybe you tell me more. Maybe no. Remember wise guy, if I no like maybe you start to think that you have accident, or have one arranged beeg shot. Who sent you?"

I said nothing.

“Come on don’t be shy. “He held out a ham size hand, pink, puffy, and packed with spots, veins, tattoos, and rings, the largest on his little finger. “Your name, maybe I hear somewhere?”

“Maybe, maybe not,” I said.

“I’m sure I know you from somewhere else, no? You are a familiar face.”

“I get that a lot. Listen Crum, we need to talk.”

“Come. Come to consultation room maybe we talk.” He stared at me for a few seconds.

“You look too tan and nice dressed for this part of town, and carry yourself like a soldier, or ex-con. Maybe someone sent you here.”

I shrugged and followed him down a dark hallway with flickering lights. There were faded diplomas on either side of the walls in some language you’d need a cryptologist to decode. “Nice office,” I lied. The consultation room at the end of the hall was illuminated by an X-ray view box and a green banker's lamp. The desk was the size of a door, on inspection it was a door. There were papers scattered and stacked, an ancient computer, and a coffee cup with pens, a wine glass and three shot glasses.

Three chairs in front of the desk were waiting for an ass to sit on. Crum squeezed into a large cushy swivel chair behind the desk, and said. "Go, go sit down and we talk."

"Sure." I sat, and waited a few beats.

"You're here you say to see patients, we know this is shit talk?"

"Yeah, seems like a promising location."

Crum laced his fingers together and rested them beneath his chin. "You sure this isn't some how you say setup?"

"That's how you say it Crum, setup."

“I think you’re cozy with the feds or lawmen no? You got some air about you that says money came and went. Fancy clothes, worn out jeans, hippy hair, tan.”

“Shit happens.”

“Maybe you tell me what you want, no?” Crum had a bottle of vodka out from who knows where and set it on the desk. “Have shot and you speak. No bullsheet. No trouble. You get this?”

“It could be trouble. I know about the house you live in on the outskirts of town. Upscale digs for an all around stooge for the big boys that front this dump. There’s been talk this is a decent place to set up a lucrative little one stop racket of a practice.”

“Who talks of me?”

“Maybe some folks who’re on to you.” I said.

“What is this talk? You check me out before coming here? Who sent you? This office space is shit talk. Stay away from my home or—”

“Or what? I’m curious. I want something from you. I did check you out, and know you’re the man. That’s why I’m here.”

“You specialized in what, family medicine bullsheet? I don’t have any stinking families coming here.”

“Gunshot wounds, particularly to the head” I mustered up my most menacing voice. It came out of a dark place and surprised me.

He poured one shot, chugged it, and poured another. “Gunshot wounds?”

“The one you have a good chance of having.”

“And you are wanting office here is shit talk isn’t it?”

"Good guess Crum. I want to make sure you don't get greedier. I know you're just a front man in this dump. I know what they need in here, and that'd be me to remind you."

He stood up. "You starting something with me big shot." His face stayed pale. "I can have my people rip out you're chest beeg shot. Nobody fock with the Zill."

"You don't have any people. I'm sure you can find some thugs, but not fast enough. And no, I'm not fuckin' with you. I have a simple one time only proposition for you."

"What is proposition?"

"You're boss has been putting the squeeze on the wrong folks. Too much attention and I'm here to tell you to patch things up through me, and ask you to lay off."

"Or what Mr. Beeg Shot?"

“Word on the street is one thing, word from the top is you’re into things that draw attention to their entire operation. You’re small-time Crum. The heavies, as in your bosses, owe me a few favors. This is one, and if they get word you may be doin’ some side deals you’re fucked.”

“Side deals? Bull sheet fucker.”

“Have you ever heard the name Romeo Royal Willens?” I let the name hang in the air, and watched his jaw twitch before he reached for the bottle of vodka.

“Out! Get the focking hell out of here now. Right now, or I’ll get you dead where you sit.”

“No you won’t. Calm down shithead. We want what you boosted from a certain courier. It isn’t mine, and until it shows up you’re going to be seeing me a lot. In fact, enough to turn this into a legit clinic, or find someone else to do it. I want you to tell your masters we’ll be around.”

He said nothing as he stared at me walking out. I hung back and listened. I heard him shout at Dixie in a tone favored by big shots, taken down a few notches. It was a desperate sober rasp with the sort of edge that slices through the air like a gunshot, a grizzly bear with one leg in a trap, and a hunter taking aim for the kill.

"Dixie, stop what you're doing and get Roy on the phone. Now." Crum was shaking.

"You can't do that Dr. Crum, ya know darn well the lines are tapped and you ain't gonna get through."

"Do what I say Dixie, or damn, shit, hell you'll be back on the street doin' tricks."

"Least I won't get killed Dr. Crum. Mr. Roy's people gonna be real mad. Who knows what they'll do."

"I know what they'll do if I don't. Now call dammit."

I heard his voice drop a few octaves. Something spooked him, and the big man was scared. And there it was. Mission accomplished. Now I could get out of this shithole.

6

LARRY THE GO BETWEEN

The car parked outside the office was a white sedan with government tags. It was idling. Its driver rolled down the window and hollered, "Get in."

The car was littered with fast-food wrappers, empty McDonald's milk shake cups, and smelled of greasy sausage, body odor, and anxiety.

"Hope you put the fix in. Smoked him out."

I buckled up in the passenger seat of the generic sedan, and said, "Larry, the guy bought it. I mustered up my best badass, and mentioned the name Romeo Roy, cowboy bartender extraordinaire."

“And a whole lot more. We’ll get back to that.” Larry put the car in gear and held his foot on the brake.

“I’m looking forward to hearing your BS.” Kurfew nodded, and rolled down his window. “Yeah, I can’t wait. I got the job done now what?”

“So far so good, that’s a start. Larry tapped his fingertips on the steering wheel and drove. “How heavy did you go?”

“I put it on. Like you said, spooked him, got a frightener goin’, when I mentioned Romeo Roy he went batshit. You set this up Larry, got me here and said you needed a favor, some unfinished business.”

“No, Thomas, I bailed you out with a warning. You’re here, and we’re off to a good first day’s work.”

“We’re not done yet?”

“No.”

“The fuck, not done yet. How deep and how long is this goin’ to take, as in how many days are you talkin’ Larry?”

“As long as it takes to get to the big guys. Why you’ve got something better to do?”

Kurfew watched the grubby scenery disappear in the sideview mirror. “Other than being watched over by you Larry I could think of a few things?”

“I’ve got to keep tabs on you. After all you did sign on for a responsibility not some cutesy favor for a favor gig when you took to layin’ low with the skirt. You knew there were strings attached, and you fucked things up. We had a contract.”

“I didn’t read the fine print.”

“Bullshit. You agreed to disappear for awhile with the goodies. Goodies that didn’t belong to you. You collected a nice piece of coin for the effort. Now my ass is on the line."

"There's that, but you set it up Mr. Hotshot. Money laundering, go-between for the Department of Defense, and every sort of scumbag on the planet. Who are you doing this for Larry, the feds, the mob, or yourself?"

"Easy Thomas. You got the pad on the beach, the money, and the stuff to sit on for a while. Did you honestly think it'd last in some happily ever after fairy tale?"

"Yeah, I did."

"You had a nice run. Now the gal's gone, and you're the usual suspect. Now Thomas you're on the hook and need to set things straight."

"And this shit is gonna get things right, huh? I'm going to needle my way into the good graces of a scumbag and his crime bosses for what, another holiday with strings attached?"

“You don’t have a choice T. If it wasn’t for me you’d be in some interrogation room, or worse.”

“How’s that Larry?”

“YOU Kurfew, are MY fucking responsibility, and that shit you were SUPPOSED to look after, the shit we handed over, the artwork and money was for a US Government slush fund to work their magic catching terrorists. It was to be kept safe, and I was the one they entrusted to do it, and I did that through you.”

“Everyone makes mistakes.”

“You were half way to becoming a full blown alcoholic down there.”

“No, I made it all the way.” Thomas slouched back on the vinyl passenger seat. “Now what?”

Larry looked at Thomas and wondered as if he was buying into this cockamamie scheme. He seemed unfocused, as if his passenger might be on to something, but dummying up and decided to string him along. Maybe lay a bit of guilt on him. So much for using a friend, if he ever was that.

"We've got to get the stuff back, find the bitch Catherine, take down the shitbird's operation, and smoke out one huge syndicate of global crumbs."

"What is this bullshit, a joke or a script for a bad movie?"

"No, it's business. Government business, and the boys upstairs have you pinned as Numero Uno scam man" Larry thumped his chest, "I vouched for you Thomas. If you don't screw it up and get this shit done we both get well, and the new government gives us a pass."

"I don't know Larry, I'm gettin' too old for this shit."

"Old enough to get killed Thomas? You just stirred the pot here on US soil."

"I thought it was a one-off. You tricked me Larry. You're acting like the criminal you are. Why are you doing this?"

"We've got to get clear of this crap Thomas. Crum's already having his handlers running a book on you. They won't find the woman that left you on Grand Cayman, but they sure's hell are gonna find you, and me. They'll figure out what to do with her, and the artwork you were supposed to look after. Shit, it was supposed to be a simple gig. And now they'll take a run at Chalkman Davis, and some of the other guys don't you get it?"

"You got popped for washing money Larry, I get it. You cut a deal with the Feds to work both sides and turn a profit. Reeled me in then and now this. I'm here Larry."

"Aside from not having anywhere to go other than wander the island boozin' it up with no broad, no money, and a cache gone bye bye?"

"We're being followed?" Thomas shifted his gaze from the sideview mirror.

"No shit, Thomas. I was banking on it." Larry checked the rearview.

"I'd rather be bumming it up on the island."

"How long would that last? Trust me, this is fat. If I don't deliver I get dumped, and you know what that means for both of us."

"Prison. I'm too pretty for Leavenworth. You'd be some chubby chaser's sweetheart."

"Fuck you Kurfew. I had a great relationship with the DOD, Homeland, Justice, and a few three letter agencies that I don't have a clue what they stand for. And now I'm a liability, so are you."

"I didn't see the rug being yanked from under me when I was on the beach."

"These guys, Crum's masters work for Roy and who knows, maybe you, or that broad you shacked up with cut a deal. The guys upstairs figure it that way." Larry took his hand off the steering wheel and pointed up. "They wanted your ass and the goodies stashed in the Caymans. I sent you the ticket out and a place to crash because you can put the team together and bring down these shitbirds."

"I've got to actually hunt down mobsters? Get outta here. Drop me off at–"

"Where? You're in this. And we share a healthy cut. You just have to stay in character."

"What did happen to the stuff?"

"Poof. The higher ups want it, but not all of it. That's where we come in. We find out where it went, we get our end, and that's it. Easy peasy. My guess, and on good intel on the street it's in the hands of the nasty shit Royal Willens, your favorite bartender."

"That prick's still breathing?"

"Thomas, Roy runs rackets in this town, and across the motherfucking world. He ripped off the US government, among others and disappeared. Uncle Sam isn't that forgiving, but you dickhead, and your former lady's high flying lifestyle got too many eyes in too many places."

"It was easy to get used to Larry. She was easy to be with. Everything was great, and now this. Why drum up old mercs and bent docs?"

"Because you're broke Thomas, on too many lists, and a liability. Moron that got taken by a shady broad. Shit, dirtbag grifters wouldn't go near you. Your judgement sucks."

"The sex was good."

"Shut your dick up and stay out of the booze cabinet. And I mean the stinkin' minibar at the dump I booked you at. Get this right and this might just make things square with the Government, the mob, medical boards, if you ever want to do that shit, and life goes on. Only this time on the up-and-up. You get that Thomas?"

"Up and up huh? Didn't think that was part of your world. What next? I've got a few yards left on some beat charge cards, and not much cash left."

"Got you covered." Larry dug into his sports coat inside pocket and handed over an envelope.

"Then what?" Thomas examined the contents. More cash, another burner, and a charge card." He held up the card, "Is this legit?"

"For the most part, yes, it's good to go. Tonight, I want you to scope out Crum's house on the outskirts. Find something we can take to the department."

"Which department is that Larry?"

There was a jolt of metal kissing metal whiplashing both men. Two armed men in paramilitary drag rushed toward them. "Shit, this ain't no fender bender. You pressed the right buttons Thomas. I'm gettin' the hell outta here. Gotta lose these schmucks."

There was a gunshot, it shattered the rear window. "Damn that was fast." Larry stared at the road ahead and punched the gas pedal.

"Larry, if they wanted us dead we'd be dead. It's a frightener for a frightener. C'mon, these are pros."

Kurfew considered that Larry may be holding his cards close, too close, and he might lead him through this maze to get a peek at his hand. Even though Larry had a long history of bluffing, and one thing was certain, the wild card was Romeo Royal Willens.

7

CHALK

He was nursing a slow beer at Molly's Menagerie Bar in Miami, staring at the booze bottles, thinking of everything and nothing. The image in the mirror behind the liquor was a silver haired black man of indeterminable age, who to Molly had that look of someone who'd seen everything and chose to forget about most of it.

"Chalk, y'all know them fellas down the end by the door?" She tossed the bar rag over her shoulder and grinned mirthlessly before whispering, "They ain't been here afore, and says they wanna buy you a drink. They friends of yours?" She stared at the faded tattoo on Chalk's left forearm. "Maybe they's enlisted men wantin' some props from an old African American soldier."

“I have a drink,” Chalk raised his glass and saw two men sipping bottled water. They were dressed in paramilitary costumes, trying but failing to project some tough boy look. He stared at the woman for a beat and said, “There was a time Molly, when you wouldn’t serve Negroes, then coloreds, then blacks, were fine. And now, African Americans are wonderful.” He stared at the scrunched features on the woman’s face.

"Bless your heart. I have to keep up with the times.” Molly said.

The two men got off their stools and wandered casually toward the silver haired man, stopping an arms length away. “Lieutenant Chalkman Davis, sir.” One of the man boys said with a smirk reserved for being shortchanged at the carnival. “They say you’re a pretty good pilot gramps.” The other stood there quietly with a calm menace reserved for bouncers at a sold out pop concert.

Chalk glanced at the mirror sizing up the two huge, but not too huge, men. They were both armed. The bulge was a rookie tell, and said "I was, a long time ago." He stared at their foreheads before standing up. "What can I do for you?"

"We need you to come with us."

"I'm busy flirting with Molly. It might take a few hours." He was scribbling a note on his napkin. "Take this Molly, and make this call after I'm gone."

"Sure gramps," staring at the scrawl.

She watched one of the young men say to Chalk, "Come on, let's get a move on."

"That's not gonna happen sonny."

Molly would later recall the silver haired man stare at the fellas. "He seemed ta know they was up to no good. No durn good at all." She'd tell what happened to the man whose number Chalk left. A man with a funny name.

Without another word the silver haired man drove his right elbow into the neck of the man speaking, and his left knee into the bouncer's nether regions. Three palm thrusts to each faster than Molly's bar rag dropped. Chalk grabbed both men by the backs of their necks and smashed them onto the Lucite counter. "Who sent you two young bloods?" He kicked both of them behind their knees fast, hard, and with the economy of motion reserved for conserving energy.

"Look at you gramps. Was you really tryin' to get frisky with me sugah?" She rearranged her beehive hair and forced a brown toothy smile. "Bless your dear heart Chalk," and squeezed the bar rag.

"Bless your heart too Molly. If anyone asks, I was never here. Get it? I want you to call that number, say I was compromised." He notched his chin to the napkin.

She took the bar rag from her shoulder and went about mopping wondering who'd pay the tab.

EVENING IN BIG TOWN: THOMAS PAYS A VISIT

8

SUBURBAN RENEWAL

On the outskirt's of Big Town is a quaint suburb on the border of tranquility and that subtle mist of oddities. A quiet place to wander around as a stranger enjoying the scenery. Eerie vistas and the sort of architecture from another time.

The townies, friendly sorts, yet that off-colored synchrony with some unseen pulse, something beneath the surface you can see behind their eyes, their ways, something menacing as if they're under some spell conspiring in hushed tones, gently drawing in strangers.

A border town on the edge of another dimension has an in-between sense of secrets, either designed to draw you in or keep you out.

An hour or so perusing the hood before the sunset had a sense of a strained quaintness with perfunctory nods of shopkeepers and local's gazes. Something was off, as if the air'd been filtered through some sort of prism. The townies had an off-colored synchrony reserved for mannequins herded by threads of obedience. There was some synchronous pulse among them, something beneath the surface behind their eyes, their ways, something menacing as if they were under some spell conspiring in hushed tones, gently drawing in strangers.

I parked a block away from the house. it was in a gated community, a subdivision, and the house was on a dead end street. I finessed my way past the security guard at the gate with a C note, he frowned at it, but snatched it up fast. I didn't notice a tail and waited. Fifteen minutes oozed by assured me no one was out and about Nothing, no one. Time to pay a visit to Dr. Crum whether he was home or not didn't matter. There was a wall with barbed wire and a rusty weathered gate. There was a CCTV camera, and a callbox. I pressed the button a few times and waited. Nothing. No answer. Tried again, and figured to jimmy the gate. Looked easy enough, maybe too easy. Five minutes into the procedure the silence of night broke with the sound of a woman's shout.

"Stop."

She was serious. Chin tucked down, strands of hair made a cage of her face, shiny eyes of some unknown hue reflected beneath the moonlight. The gun, a Sig Sauer P229 pistol. Some kind of government training. The modified Weaver stance was perfect. Slightly bent knees and figured if she was gonna shoot I'd already be dead. But that wasn't going to happen.

"Why are you here?" Her voice sounded like velvet dragged over fine sandpaper.

"Sightseeing," I raised my hands. "I was looking at some real estate."

Her accent had a hint of Great Britain, and a spray of freckles across her nose. Sculpted cheekbones, and cut of her face. She wore a black tank top beneath a man's sport's coat and jeans that muted her frame, but not by much. I couldn't sprint back to the rental car, maybe I didn't want to.

She knew that. The narrowed eyes and knuckles on the pistol's grip shined in the moonlight. "It's been a while Thomas."

She lowered the gun, took a few steps toward me, brushed stray hairs away from her face and tucked them behind her ear. She shoved the gun into the back of her jeans beneath the uniform, and put her arms around my waist. Her body was firm and she had the smell of mischief. It was a briny sweet smell, hypnotic, disarming, and something I couldn't put my finger on, but thought hard about trying to.

She had a slight limp, and took out a pack of cigarettes, looked at it, and decided against.

"Maybe you're working an angle lady, your own shakedown without the lawyer Larry?"

"Wasn't he disbarred in this country?" Her accent was gone. "Whatever."

"I can tell by the accent gambit you're up to something," waited a beat and said, "Maybe we both are." Her eyes had hints of amusement and perhaps, more than a touch of danger

"Maybe. I was washing Dr. Crum's car and had you followed from the office. You may have thought you lost the tail this morning. That bump was to throw you off."

"Those tough boys were what, stooges Sea Witch? What does that make you?"

"What does it make me? Mysterious. Isn't that what drives a man mad? The boys were hires to keep eyes on Crum." She clammed up for a beat. "Dixie had me stay at the house. If you want a tour," she stepped back and held the sack out as a tease. "Maybe you can say you were swept off your feet by the architecture. No?"

"I think we're both after the same thing, but from different points of view." I wouldn't have noticed the sack, an old Seagram's booze bag, of something that rattled. If she didn't bite down on her lower lip, and smile a silly lopsided grin and deep clear your throat chuckle I wouldn't have taken that tingle seriously. "You're offering me a tour, eh? That you'd do this for me is adorable. You do this for all of Crum's visitors?"

"Only the ones that might get his boss put away, deported, or some unsavory recognition."

"C'mon, he's a nice guy. For a short con hustler that runs a nice operation."

"Crum and his mates are nothin' but barney." The accent stung my ears and itched the way a song from my past hits that certain chord over and over. It was a beautiful song

"I reckon so Meredith. You do clean up well."

"You know those aren't pills in the sack Thomas. That sort of an operation has to keep guys like Crum on a short leash."

"But you knew that, didn't you?"

"Actually our dear Larry did when he rescued us off the coast of Grand Cayman, played along with his act, and showed up at Crum's office," she tapped the bag, "The people Crum work with want you dead."

"There's a waiting list."

"I'm sure there is Thomas. I'm not on it." She paused, "Yet."

That playful jubilant persiflage spelled trouble in a language I'd forgotten, and trouble these days is a hobby I'd have to relearn.

We strolled arm in arm to and through Crum's home. I didn't know where anything was, or where to start looking. The place was arranged like a maze. A puzzle she seemed to know well, and pointed out a few items before we rested on a sofa where she draped herself across the deep oxblood leather. It was the kind of sofa that swallowed you whole, built to impress with its solid frame and plush cushions she leaned forward, stood, snatched a liquor bottle and two crystal glasses from an elaborate bar, and poured me a drink .

"I know you're working an angle. You don't seem to be the sort of woman who'd take orders from anyone."

"I didn't say who I take orders from," she said notching her head toward the bedroom. "Tell me what sort of woman I am?"

"The sort that gets under my skin and stays there. Maybe this is a setup."

She moved closer until our faces touched and hands wandered across each other and we kissed, a tooth clattering tongue twisting kiss. My chest ached with each systolic burst.

I don't know what happened next. I awoke tied to a chair. My last recollection was a sip of water, after that things went blank. The light trickled in through the blinds, a breeze from the ceiling fan rustled the note taped to the mirror. I put some oomph into clenching and releasing my wrists maybe wrangle out of this and realized through the fog how gently the ties were applied, and the taste of her kiss lingered. Too weak, too hazy, and too blind to see if I'd been duped or drawn in. I rocked the chair to read the note, and dozed off wondering what it meant.

The note read:

No pills or pebbles in Seagram sack. Stones, Painite. Musgravite. Bixbite, Red Beryl the rest is yours. Meet in Florida ASAP.

What the fuck was she into, the layover in Miami, then this? Shit, what was I into? Something smelled rotten, and it took a few minutes to realize it was the corpse of Zillonious Crum on the floor. I drifted off into a dreamless sleep.

TWO DAYS EARLIER: MEREDITH MEETS EDDY IN MIAMI

9

EDDY

Where the fuck was that broad? I'm a busy guy, and the stinking airport pickup was loaded with cops waving people to move their cars, hollering, and all the douchebag tourists and their kids running around whining about lost luggage. Some friend, calls out of the blue. Needs to help this girlfriend can I be there? Of course I'm there. Pick up at airport. Sure, no problem. Dickhead Kurfew's woman. Where the freakin' hell was that shithead? Said he had some "special" don't ask issues brought from Grand Cayman. He's no dope's so it sure wasn't anything that'd get him pinched, or me. But it had to be something worth draggin' me out on account he may've been in some kind of jam. Shit, a cop was rapping on my hood with a baton. What the?

"You're gonna have to move along or get towed," he waved his arm the way someone'd flick phlegm they'd coughed up. I put the ride in gear and oozed into the flow of traffic. Shithead Kurfew said she needed my attention. Mind you, I'm a busy man, I had appointments and it was gettin' late. My watch didn't work, but I checked it anyway for the benefit of any other car jam copper and waved as if I gave a shit. An hour of driving around the perimeter road and back to passenger pickup. Nada.

The broad caught my eye

I'd met her once, thought I did, maybe a while back maybe maybe not. She was standing at Cayman Air's passenger pickup station waving, Was she waving at me? She matched the description Kurfew gave me, vague as it was, she had something Thomas was attracted to that natural good but not fashion model look, and fuck-all grace some women carry and others drop. He had good taste.

Something about her, something exotic. She moved as if no one existed in the space she occupied, like she was surrounded by some invisible shield. Not a bad lookin' broad. Nice shape, sorta smokin' in that Palm Beach chi-chi way. She wore a scarf that looked more like a rag, designer shades, tan under a flimsy make that worn T-shirt; and a bandage on her leg. I pulled over, honked and said."You're definitely not Catherine?"

"You must be his idiot friend Edward?" She tossed a cigarette to the ground looked at him and thought. They weren't good thoughts.

"At your service good lookin'."

"We meet," Eddy stared at her tanned face and worked his way down. Shit, she didn't have a bra on, and that outfit made her shape stand out the way a .... Eh, never mind. "You needed a ride Thomas said you had a wound needing a look see, right?"

"What do you think Edward?"

"Had to ask. You got any luggage?"

“Just this,” she notched her head at a bag on wheels. Some kind of backpack purse .

“Where’s my man Thomas?” I had my eyes on her chest as she leaned in.

“He was supposed to be here by now. He had to check in with a guy downtown. That was two hours ago. I couldn’t reach him, and he said if I needed to find him you’d know how Edward.”

“The shithead doesn’t carry a phone!”

“He’s funny that way,” she shrugged.

“That dunsky. What shit’s he got goin’ on these days?”

“He doesn’t say much.”

“Where are you stayin’?”

“South county, some hotel outside of town. Thomas said you were a bit of a wanker.”

"Kurfew said to take care of you, and he'd come around later. Buckle up. Whatever your name is. "You must be his new squeeze now that Catherine's gone."

She ran her hand over the dashboard, adjusted the air conditioning, "Bangin' Aston Martin Edward. Posh car for a bloke with a tongue from the street."

"Lighten up lady, you want a ride or not?"

"Observant aren't we? Shall we get on with things Edward?"

"Things as in your wound and that's it. Anything else today honey?"

Damn, what've I gotten into. Been friends with Kurfew for years, med school, army, residency. Shit, I owed him enough for a simple favor. Then again the last favor nearly got me killed. Picking up this lovely with a limey accent, what harm is there to that?

“Don’t call me honey.”

“Sweetie, do you have any idea where Thomas is at?”

“Not exactly, and don’t call me sweetie. He said he had to meet someone, an old friend.” She lied.

“When was the last time you saw him?”

“Hours ago Edward, we came in by seaplane, cab dropped me here. Thomas said you and the blokes on board were mates.”

“What else did he say?”

“Not much. He mention anything besides the shape of my boobs?”

“He said your name was Meredith and whatever you had going on was done, and needed to get off the island. Something about being in deep shit, finding his ex-lady, and a whole lot of stolen ... Some shit about people wanting him dead."

"It's complicated Edward." She looked to her side and spoke softly "Eddy, I'm not here on holiday. You're charm is wasted, but my leg needs tending to, and you're the bloke for tending. Call me in some antibiotics, or drop me at a proper practitioner's office." She pointed her nose at Eddy. "I'd say that I'm sorry for this, meet and greet but back off you're in over your head Edward."

"I'm a board certified plastic surgeon lady, and have a full free standing outpatient clinic. And that's where we're going?"

"No, we're not. You are going to tell me what you did involving Catherine's disappearance."

"That's confidential." He pulled the car into a parking space in Miami International's garage. "I'm not going anywhere until I find out what the hell's going on lady?"

"We'll see about that," her tone was firm.

"What the ... ?" Something about the way she spoke. It was as if she knew where I'd be, and was using me to blindside Thomas. "Who the fuck are you? I thought Thomas was drinking himself to oblivion over that thing he had after some score. Thought he had it made in paradise, happy crappy forever shit."

"You thought wrong Edward." She slowly reached into her handbag, and in one continuous motion removed a tiny syringe that was within a lipstick container jabbed him with a needle and pressed down on the plunger. Seconds later Eddy was woozy. Fifteen minutes passed and Eddy's description vividly described anything and everything he knew, and more she tucked away to use against him. After another ten minutes she returned to the passenger pick-up. A white sedan with government tags was waiting, honked and Meredith got in.

Edward Arthur Vinnetti, M.D. worked his way toward consciousness with a sluggish stealth of awareness, thoughts scattering, none of them made sense. He served with Kurfew as combat surgeons over a dozen years ago. Both were less than willing soldiers, and Eddy who'd shortened his name by then was paying off student loans for his ticket to med school and an entry into a plastic surgery residency. When Thomas intervened replacing Eddy to throw in with a band of mercenaries Eddy wanted no part of it. It was Thomas who saved him from going into the dark world of things nobody gets anywhere from, and Eddy was not going to get caught up in that. He had a career back home.

"Edward Vincent." The cop who'd flicked snot off his finger was standing next to the car when Eddy awoke barely aware he'd been approached by police, thinking he may have dreamt hearing, "License and registration."

"How much have you had to drink sir?"

"Nothing, I don't drink, I was drugged."

Twelve hours and a few thousand dollars in lawyering later the fog lifted, the puncture wound on his neck had closed, and the dope showed up in the lab results.

Eddy had no idea if, under the influence, he spilled the beans on Kurfew, the meet and greet in Big Town, the rat-shit Larry, and the shake-down. Whatever it was she extracted Eddy thought may be exactly what Thomas wanted. He was certain TK could handle it.

10

SPOOKY

A marauding squad of tattooed Millennials, Gen Z'er's, or whatever, surrounded the 1979 Rolls-Royce Corniche with the top down, texting like mad birds at an empty bag of peanuts. One of them raised his gaze and stepped toward the man heading their way with keys in hand.

The stench of crystal meth carried hard in the humid, early evening breeze. A semi-tough boy said: "Sweet ride Slick, now gimme your wallet," A smartphone aimed at the chest.

"Slick?" The man in the fedora waited a beat, considered bashing the kid's head in, but was too tired. He opted to say, "You got bullets in that phone? Must not be in the right neighborhood for smartphone ammo." He kept walking thinking these bums and their shit are either part of a setup or stupid. After all, it was the Island, the place where old and new presidents golf, and dead Kennedys haunt Worth Avenue.

There were no cops, there never are unless you've got the music amped up, or a guy without his shirt on. "Whoa," shoving the shopping cart between him and the iPhone as the others surrounded them A flock of knuckleheads doin' their thing remotely. It was, after all hard times in chi-chi town, and judging by the tweaker's gaze the only thing on this kids face was terminal acne. There was a woman there, barely that, He could smell her ovulating. She faked a yuck that'd make a Kardashian fart Froot Loops.

"I don't carry a stinking wallet," stroked his goatee and aimed it at the stoners. "You want a piece of me huh? You know who I am?" Putting on his best authoritative voice considering the tire iron he kept wedged beneath the driver's seat, but too wiped out from his busy day to fetch.

"Yeah," the ovulator hopped off her perch. "A real nobody in the wrong town."

"Which town do I belong in dipshit?" He looked at his watch. "`Bout ten seconds y'all're gonna find out what the word gettin' popped means."

"Screw you." Tat boy looked at the man, the old Rolls, then back at the guy in the straw fedora.

"And that'd be," he pointed a finger, then another in what one of the tweakers would later recall as a backwards peace sign.

"Two. that would be two cops. Count `em."

The few times the cops did show up at the parking lot at the market were when some shoplifting was called in by a law abiding citizen. And the shoplifter was grinning as if he'd gotten away with something, and flashed a diamond studded front tooth when the burst of a suppressed siren hushed as it is in that part of town whispered hard. The officer behind the wheel rolled down his window, looked at the kids, nodded and said “Welcome back Mr. Pollack, sir. I take it you made the shoplifter call.”

“Yes, I did.” He stroked his goatee and shrugged. “Just a concerned citizen officer.”

Harold Spooky Pollack inherited his uncle’s Palm Beach Estate. H P the Great, a jazz legend who not only jammed and recorded with the greats, but won gold records. He left behind more than just the lavish house on South Ocean Drive. The inheritance included an aging Rolls Royce convertible, a vintage Selmer saxophone, and a pimped-out spiffy wardrobe. He also passed along more than the home. Spooky inherited years of disrepair, back taxes, gambling debt, and his late uncle’s profligate ways. Spooky maintained his front as a hotshot wheeler dealer despite having no visible means of support, or so it seemed, if his life depended on it, and it did. Romeo Roy and his crew reminded him of certain obligations he had down on Grand Cayman for some cash owed because he had the bad habit of betting on the wrong horse in the right race. The gambling gene put him in so deep he had to consider options.

Spooky, when he thought of himself, the image of a carefree high-roller hotshot man-about-town was in jeopardy of being exposed. After all he survived financially by short cons, heavy betting, quick insurance scams, and shadowy deals buried in the nobody's bizz corner of his mind. The threat to his facade popped up when he'd have issues, either with the law, a grift gone sour, or a bad bet might get him banished from the circuit. But that was the least of his worries. At the moment he knew he was in a jam with conditions that he might be able to skate on, but if things went south, he might be in for some serious bodily injury or a dirt nap

The cracks in his facade became obvious, and he would have to abstain from showing up at the Lingling Bar to knock back shots of tequila, and jam out on stage. The audience hoping he could belt out riffs like The Great H P, left puzzled that despite his efforts the Spook man couldn't blow through the reeds without a ventilator. He needed help, and maybe a little more time. So he thought of himself, and didn't like the image of broken bones, or a sudden case of death. He became vividly aware of old Uncle H P, who'd come up as an icon before the term African American became part of the lexicon. It would remind him that being black in America had challenges money and fame couldn't overcome. What Spooky needed now was a score, a maneuver of sorts, that'd get him out from under a heavy debt, and the only guys he could think of to pull it off were in the nowhere to be found zone.

Chomping down on the snacks he boosted from the market he dusted off the seat of the car, and set out on making the right calls to the wrong people. Among them was his Uncle Chalk, hotshot pilot, ex-military, a finger in everything, and nothing in his hands. The guy with connections. He'd know what to do, put me in touch with some feds or law sorts. He'd heard about that fucking no where to be found Kurfew, and how he finessed his way into fat city. Unc told him about the fatso contact at the State Department Larry Kaminsky. Those guys always needed information. Spooky never considered himself a rat, but under the prevailing circumstances a bit of cheese seemed appetizing.

He eased the Rolls up the driveway to find a car with government plates, and a woman, hands on her hips, glowing in the headlights. She seemed to the best of Spooky's recollection alone, and put the car in park. He opened the door tire iron in his right hand and began to ooze out of the vehicle when a firm grip squeezed his shoulder. "Harold, try not to piss that sporty white suit."

"Meredith. That was a quick move. Pleasure to see you again, wanna let go of my arm?"

"Posh crib you have here Harold." She released her grip and stepped back. "Put that away, you should've beaten those bloody bum fuckers with it in the parking lot." She eyed the tire iron as if it was a limp snake, maybe something a bit more naughty.

“Didn't wan’t 5-0 on me for assault with a deadly weapon.” Spooky gazed at the crowbar on the ground and shifted his gaze on the woman.

“Oh, that’s what happened Harold. Bullshit.”

“You’ve been following me.” Spooky eyed her, shook his head, and grinned. “Who are you lady?”

“We’re on the same side Harold. Difference is I have better connections.”

“Are we?” Spooky stared at her sculpted face.

“We both want a piece of Roy Willens. You’ve you’re reasons, I’ve mine.”

“How’s that?”

“At the bar down on Grand Cayman you were pretty cozy with Romeo Roy Willens. What the fuck. His errand boy, tryin’ to work off a debt or run an angle? You know he'd have you killed if he thought you were running a scam."

"What the fuck are you runnin' lady? Dammit. You got Kurfew off the island."

"Damn straight I did. He's on to the stash, or at least picked up the scent, and that will lead us right to it.

"Us? Meredith, what's in it for you?"

"I want the rest of the Lucite counter embedded coins, then I want the rest, maybe it's personal. When I do get it I want that cowboy Romeo Roy's arse dead or alive."

"With what army Meredith? That shit's gone. Roy had it torn out and stashed on that yacht of his, and that boat's a fortress."

"No shit Spooky, and most likely to have the stash on board."

"A boat?"

"It's a two hundred sixty footer with a gray hull, and angular lines that reduce its radar profile, and a military grade double helipad. It's docked offshore Miami.

"How do you know this?"

"I'm quite resourceful Harold, surely you've noticed."

"Surely." Spooky couldn't tell if she was some sort of law, on the grift, or something else.

"Spooky, either you're with me on this, or on your own, broke, a step away from a serious beat down, and jail. And you do know what they do to a grass in prison?"

"Grass? I'm not a rat." Even though Spooky gave it some serious consideration. "However, if there's something in it for me I can contribute to your, uh, whatever it is your after."

“Then you’re going to get us on board that boat. You still have an in with the cowboy, right?”

“I do this and that for him.”

“Peachy, so we’re all set. I’ve a long drive, and a plane to catch.”

“I don’t know. Me being here with you, who knows Roy might’ve set up that rendezvous with those kids in the parking lot.”

“I set that up you plonker.”

“Hey cool it. I’m no fool lady, and you, shit, you’ve got more connections than a Mexican nuclear power plant.”

“And then some.”

“Between Kurfew, your kin Chalk, and the fat clown Larry, we’re good to go,” yawning. “Must be off now Harold it’s been wonderful. Here’s a burner answer it, or if something comes up call me.It's the only number on speed-dial."

Harold Spooky Pollack removed his straw fedora and scratched his head wondering if this Sally Brown might beat him with a cukumaka stick. He stared at the phone before slipping it into his pocket.

KURFEW TIED UP OUTSIDE OF BIG TOWN: REBOUNDING

11

The first time you almost die Kurfew thought, is scary. The second time, you feel lucky. By the third time you get a sense that your luck's run out. You say F-it and fear evaporates because you've already accepted you may not see the next sunrise. This wasn't one of those days.

I wasn't weak and hazy anymore, just dehydrated and headachy with excoriated wrists from whatever crap whatever her name had used to tie me up with. My head would've ached if I gave a shit, but the stiff in the room put me in the red zone. I could be lookin' at a murder rap if I didn't work this out, and figured the sea witch arranged it that way. I couldn't accept it, no, the smell of her, and the stench of Crum's remains.

I could hear the ceiling fan whomp whomp whomp like an Apache Gunship. The light wasn't shining through the blinds, and my mouth tasted like the bottom of a bird cage. But her smell, overrode death and that's something that tickled my amygdala.

How long was I out? Thoughts ran through my mind with static secrets. It seemed like a day would last for a week. And shit, the woman, the boat, the days in Miami, formed shapes and puzzle pieces that didn't fit. Why the note about rare stones. Who was Meredith?

Sure's hell not what I'd expected. Expecting is one of my dumbass processes to get shit done. Calculate the variables, the possible trajectories, things that could go wrong, and for the most part, managed things that went wrong. My second ex-wife, my malpractice suits, tossing in with those shitbird mercenaries back then, and a trip from a top notch practice to a low life desk jockey. How did she know about the bag of stones? I'd been set up. Something hit me hard on the back of my head, and consciousness evaporated faster then the few bucks I'd pawned my watch for.

I heard a whisper. "Thomas, go back to sleep." It wasn't a woman's voice. My wrists ached as if the restraints were tightened, and a click of a lock before things faded to black.

The fan was still slicing the air when I awoke.

Eddy was supposed to meet me. Shit, he doesn't know where the fuck I am, or why, or anything about the lift, or maybe he was in on it. Nah, not Eddy. We'd been classmates for years. Both of us did our residencies at the same hospital. Hung out for years, even spent some time in the dark side of merc work together. He figured there was more to lose chasing and being bad guys, and more to gain, a whole lot more in plastic surgery. Eddy, greedy shitbird. Private military companies were too much for him. Nothing more than death whores. He preferred the living breathing ones, especially any–as he'd say, smokin' broad' to scratch his itch. Eh, I did too, and maybe a part of me got myself into this, and now, if my head starts clearin' I can wrangle out of this.

I started rocking the chair, maybe break it, and my wrists being shriveled up, work my way out of this, or better yet get to the Swiss Army knife in the right pocket of my jeans. Shit, that'd be a position to get in, but fuckit. I started rocking harder thrusting my shoulders toward my knees, like I was doing sit ups, and felt the hand ties loosen and the knife start to poke out onto my belly and tumble onto the tile floor.

I'd been making progress. Things were becoming possible, or maybe I was zoning out, but I heard something, and it was loud enough to send waves of pain through my head. Shit. The door, some asshole was banging on it, the sure's hell didn't have a key or think of using the window, and I got to figure it was Crum's lackeys or the local cops ... or shit, maybe the chick was back. Any way I tried to figure I'd have some explainin' to lie about.

There was a voice, deep, baritone, throaty, and sounded like it came from the bottom of an oil drum.

"Thomas, Thomas, Thomas," sounded more like dumbass dumbass dumbass. I knew that voice. Fucking Larry Kaminsky.

"Notice Crum's body Thomas?"

"Yeah," I was rubbing my wrists. "Stinks like shit."

"There's open wounds, incisions, c'mon take a look, you're a doctor."

I inspected the body. The belly distended, ascites, a Rand McNally Roadmap of blood vessels crisscrossed his pasty flesh. There were areas on his lower abdomen which had been previously sutured, and now gaping. As if something was removed. "Larry, he had some shit sewed under his skin."

"This shit stinks I gotta barf," Larry stepped away from the body, paced and rambled. "I read the note Thomas, and my guess it was worth stealing."

"Larry, he would've been dead soon. The gut, the spider veins, jaundice. Shit he was a serious day-drinker, probably end stage liver disease."

Thomas didn't mention the coins, Krugerrands, Pandas, and cash, Crum stashed at the house he'd found with the woman. A few in his corpse, and pocketed.

"Cool it Larry. Listen, I went through what happened before I passed out, the woman, and the booze bag. She's into something, and I don't have a clue." Kurfew had more than a clue, he knew without knowing.

"I'm pretty sure there's a whole lot more to Meredith Larry."

"So what. This is big Thomas." Larry reread the note "bigger than anyone'd think. Those gemstones if they're for real they make VVS1 diamonds look like chump change."

"I've been chasing shadows since you engineered this Larry, the shell corporations, the stolen art you conned me into holding on to, and now this shit? What's in it for me?"

"Shut up Thomas, Red beryl? Do you know what that's worth? And how about the other stones the commie had packed in that lard belly."

"Did you find anything else worth finding?" Larry narrowed his eyes.

"I didn't look too hard, being unconscious does that Larry."

"What's in it for you? Shithead, I put trackers in your burn phone, the car, another in that Swiss Army Knife. What's in it is you get out of jail." He paused a few beats. "Maybe a few Shekels."

"Get your ADD under control Larry. There was something about the way the tissues were layered to form pouches, and the scarring dates the wounds way back. Someone had to be trained, as in seriously trained could do this. And no way Meredith could've ."

"Anyone come to mind among your circle of surgeon thieves."

"We all can't be upstanding go-betweens like you Larry."

"Ha. I should have listened to my mother and gone to podiatry school."

"What do we do with the body, our prints, DNA, the crime scene cops'll be here. I can torch the place."

Shaking his head, "No fires. You've gotta get that `worked with mercenaries' shit outta your head. Shit, I got it covered. I am an attorney Thomas. Let's get the fuck outta here."

"Disbarred, Larry."

"Suspended smart-ass. I'm gonna drop you off at the hotel, nobody's looking for you yet."

"Yet? Are you fuckin' nuts Larry? There's a dead guy whose dipshit office I was at—"

"It gets worse Thomas. You need to know, as of now you've got two murders on your growing rap sheet."

"Who's the other?"

"Catherine. You're on Interpol's hit list. You did have a dramatic departure from the island Thomas. There are plenty of witnesses."

"I guess that shootout and fire at the dock raised some concerns."

"And that just popped into your thick skull?"

"What's done is done. I'm hungry, do we have time to grab some take-out on the way?"

Larry pulled up a sleeve and glanced at his watch. "We got time, sure."

"Larry, that watch, it's a gold on gold Rolex, and you weren't wearing it on the seaplane, or in the car at Crum's office. It looks like the watch I sold to the bartender. Lemme see it Larry."

"You're paranoid Kurfew, I've had this since my first arms deal. A Panamanian I set up. A company in the Bahamas gave it to me."

"Bullshit," Kurfew grabbed his hand, bent his fingers, and brought Larry to his knees. "Show me the inscription on the watch."

"You're hurtin' me man, ease up." He unclasped the wristwatch, and Thomas slid it across Larry's hand. Holding it up he saw the initials, TK.

"You wanna be murder three Larry?"

"Okay okay, it was the broad. What's her tits, Meredith. She left it here. She must've because it was on the counter with the gems and shit. I snatched it, and thought maybe it was part of the Crum collection shit," rubbing his fingers. "You don't have to go nuts over a stinking watch, you want it, here take the fuckin' watch. I'll be in the car. Cops are gonna be here any minute."

"Nuts, huh Larry?" Kurfew considered Larry's voice go high and tinny, shortness of breath and flushed face. There might be some veracity to his schpiel, but not much. After all his thoughts weren't processing for the time being. "Sure, maybe things aren't making sense right now."

***

I didn't mention Eddy, and maybe should have. He was a plastic surgeon in Miami. We did some work together in the day, and stayed in touch, especially when Catherine wanted a complete makeover. Maybe he wanted something more from her, maybe there was more. Back then I would've cared, now though, she was dead to me.

Eddy made a point of wanting to bury cash in the Islands and had a fit when I told him the Cayman Islands were as secret as any US bank. He didn't get it. The ten month prison sentence put him in the red, and was doing Botox marathons to pay his rent. Any favor I'd ask was gonna cost. And right now I needed to assemble a team, put the gears in motion, and this shit-hole soon to be crawling with L E O with too many questions wasn't it. I'd have Larry drop me off at the dump near the airport to make arrangements. I was heading to Florida.

12

FLORIDA: AT THE HOTEL

The Boca Raton, formerly known as the Boca Raton Resort & Club is sandwiched between a private beachfront and the Intercostal Waterway. It has a harbor side marina with full-service slips accommodating vessels up to 150 feet. Too tight for larger boats, yet it's location on Lake Boca Raton is ideal for an easy hop on a fast boat to the Atlantic Ocean.

The resort made for the ideal meeting place, thirty minutes to Palm Beach an hour from Miami. An ideal position to develop and execute a plan. Maybe to 'borrow,' rent, or finagle a seaworthy vessel.

The three bedroom suite at the seaside hotel overlooked the Boca Inlet and the Atlantic Ocean. The sitting area anointed with high end furnishings was as Kurfew would recall, an overpriced showroom for schmucks. Which, he considered himself once in good company thereof.

Eddy was sprawled out on the sofa, the shower was running, and Thomas stared at the mini-bar.

"She didn't have to interrogate me Thomas, shit, that dope she shot me with gave me a heavy buzz and friggin' hangover from hell."

"Had to be done E. She's like that, thorough. Knew our shitbird friends'd be watching before her getaway."

"I'm not a friggin' marmaluke Thomas, you might've mentioned something about the broad bein' in on this," he pointed his nose toward the bathroom, "Slick broad. I still don't trust her."

There was a tap at the door, "Must be Chalk." Thomas let him in and returned to the sofa. "Want anything from room service, lunch, late breakfast?"

“I’m fine,” the silver haired pilot wore a dark suit, white shirt, and red tie. “Hot out there, maybe something cold.”

Meredith came out of the bathroom in a terrycloth robe rubbing her hair with a towel and shot a freshly fondled glance at Kurfew, and a once-over at Chalk, turned and spoke, “Are we set to rope in the marks?”

“I wouldn’t call them that.” Kurfew noticed her eyes darting, missing nothing, yet revealing little.

“Why’s that Thomas?” She joined him on the sofa, tucked a strand of shoulder length hair behind her ear.

“Because, Chalk said fetching a beer from the mini, “Like the man said, we’re not grifters, and I’m not sure who’s screwing who.” He sat and looked at the woman. “Isn’t that right missy? Doping Edward, the punks at the bar in Miami?”

"What was that about?" Eddy added.

"Sorry about that Eddy, I didn't want to break character. The punks work for Roy. Chalk, he's got people everywhere, they were sent to fetch you. I get it, none of us trusts anyone, even each other."

"Thomas, Chalk, and me go way back Meredith," Eddy got to his feet and staggered to nab himself a beer."

Thomas rubbed his chin. "Meet Meredith, she's cashiered Interpol E."

"Like the friggin' FBI or some three letter agency shit?"

"No E, they're not agents, they don't arrest anyone, carry guns, officially that is, but sure as shit are plugged in. They connect with every shade of law enforcement, liaison among agencies, gather intel, investigate, and coordinate. They're a huge database with serious shit connections she can tap into."

“Thomas, I don’t wanna know how you you hooked up with this broad, or why’s she in this?”

“I’m right here Edward, you can ask me anything.” She crossed her bare legs one atop the other, and tugged the robe down.

“Why bother ‘Meredith, if that is your real name, it’d be bullshit anyways.” Eddy sipped his beer.

“Here’s the skinny,” Thomas stood and scanned the room. “The big fish is Royal Willens, aka Romeo, the ‘cowboy’ and his BS bar on Grand Cayman, He was hip to the stash of fine art Larry K roped me and Catherine into, and squirreling it away offshore.”

Meredith added, “The insurance company heist. The bent blokes hired mercenaries, paid them with fine art, art stolen by the Nazis, to murder patients, make it look like suicides, that didn’t go well. Thomas got a whiff of the scam. He had worked with the mercs, in the past and got sucked in. Larry acted as a go-between for the US DOJ, but he got greedy when it came time to do his job of turning the spoils over. He set up another layer of companies, phony shell corporations, got greedier. Larry Kaminsky attorney at law couldn't move the goods. He needed Roy, the cowboy hotshot with billions. There was a Red Notice from Interpol."

Meredith took a deep breath and continued, "Catherine and Thomas had a thing," Meredith shot Kurfew a narrow pair of eyes, "but that was phony, sure they mixed it up, but she was in it for the something more than the art and money."

"Hang on, I'm confused." Eddy finished his beer. "So Catherine vanishes, runs off with the goods with this Roy mastermind jerkweed. What's the more part?"

"Something valuable Edward, and he'll stop at nothing to get what he wants. Don't underestimate the man, he's outmaneuvered the top cops and crooks for years."

"Eddy, Chalk, hear her out. When she was with Interpol she had access to Roy's ties with Larry and a cache of data she could've had him popped."

"Hold on, Thomas." Chalk stared at her. "She bums a flight off Grand Cayman as a Brit low life, shows up for a Q and A with Eddy, and now she's a bounty hunter. Isn't that right missy?"

She locked eyes, with the seated silver haired pilot, drew her lips in, and waited before saying, "In a manner of speaking."

"For who?" Eddy rubbed his neck.

"My bloody self." Meredith tightened her robe.

"Guys," Thomas broke into a command voice, "Larry set us all up, with Roy's help. I went along with him, the prick was too hungry to see through my drunken sad sack routine and kept dropping hints. Phony bastard. There was no government deals, Larry was on the edge of jail time, or getting offed by Roy's boys. Dumb shit."

Eddy took a sip of beer. "So what about our plan for reappropriating, and dividing the old masters, and that special 'something else' four ways Thomas?"

"I'm working on it." Kurfew took a vodka from the minibar unscrewed the cap and tossed it back in one gulp. "They're on the armor coated yacht, a floating art gallery, where he sells off piece by piece to collectors around the world. He finances armies, buys weapons and whores, dope, you name it, every criminal enterprise goes for untraceable currency and crypto's gone sour. The something special we deal with later."

Meredith perked up and spoke in a tone reserved for dirty cops, prison guards, and game wardens, "With Catherine presumed dead, Roy, and Chalk's nephew, Harold Spooky Pollack, they're converting the art to precious gems. Their worth billions, easy to transport across borders, and cowboy Roy knows someone's on to him. That makes us all targets."

"That makes us shitbird Larry's dancing monkeys." Thomas tossed the empty in a Lebron dunk toward an Art Deco trash can, and missed.

"Thomas, before we met at the docks, when I was still stalking Romeo Roy I was at the bar. The cheap Lucite counter embedded with coins, they weren't phony, they were Roy's hiding place, one of them anyway. That's why I was there. Turning it over to my former employer was less profitable than tossing in with the likes of you guys." Her accent was pure midwest USA, no BS nada. "When I met Thomas at Crum's house I planted some stones to lure Larry in. It worked. We set the stage for Larry to lead us to Roy."

"And my moron nephew?" Chalk reached for another beer. "He's either in over his head to hang on to the Palm Beach mansion, or going for the big score. Idiot. He should have stuck with the sax and a good whoopin' from Roys boys. How did you know about the gems missy?"

She said nothing. Kurfew saw the eyes tighten, and a quick wrinkle of the brow. Micro-expressions come on fast and disappear faster. They're handy tells, flash on a face, maybe stress often calculation. She's not gonna bluff Chalk.

"Go on, tell him Meredith, he needs to know." Kurfew said.

"I did visit Spooky, I told him I searched the house. He was scared. He knew about the Lucite counter and where it was. It's on—"

"His boat." Kurfew finished her sentence. "You're sure about that Meredith?"

"You drug him too lady?" How do we board, do our thing, and boogie?" Eddy said.

"Good question E," Thomas smiled. "We're going to be invited."

***

The first shot cracked the window, sliced through the air followed by a second, then a third, each echoing off the walls of the suite like a desperate plea for attention. Then came sharp staccato bursts shattering the window into spiderweb patterns, large jagged pieces falling inward sounding like beer bottles smashing on a tile floor. The sound of breaking glass was a symphony of chaos, an entropic rage in a discordant melody that sent everyone into an adrenaline rush.

"Hit the motherfucking dirt," Chalk hollered.

Shards of glass littered the room, glinting ominously in the daylight like burning stars. The jagged window looked like a gaping mouth, as if it was in shock, For Chalk, Eddy, and Thomas, they'd heard it before. The walls bore pock marks near the ceiling. Dark stains where bullets struck had a message. They weren't meant to kill, rather remind they were on notice.

“If that’s an invitation no RSVP from me.” Chalk looked at Kurfew.

“Thomas, who’s pickin’ up the tab for this friggin’ room?”

“Shut the fuck up Eddy. I put it on one of Larry’s charge cards. Go scan the waterways for the shooter.”

“Who’d do this?” Meredith studied the wounded walls. “Nine millimeter slugs, nicely placed. Some marksmanship. They were pros.”

“They teach you that in Interpol school lady? Hear the sirens, we’ve gotta boogie.” Eddy short of breath back from the terrace. “I’m not sticking around for a Q and A with law enforcement.”

“Local police? Give them twenty minutes or so after they go through the red tape at the hotel.” Chalk brushed glass chips aside. “

“He’s right, anyone have a cigarette?” She stood, patted her robe, and shrugged in the absence of nicotine. "The local cops won't do shit, they'll ask some questions, write it up, and waste some time. I can handle that. My Interpol ID comes in handy."

"Like that UK passport Meredith? Lay it on thick for John Q, we don't want anyone sniffing around. You're a tourist on holiday."

"Please Thomas, I'm not a bloody muppet mate. What will you be doing? You can tell me, we are on the same side, aren't we?" She pulled him toward her, and hugged him hard. "That is your phone pressing against me, isn't it?" She didn't blush.

"E, Chalk and me are going for a ride. You arrange for another suite, they'll comp it Meredith. Anything else put on Larry's tab."

13

A FEW MILES INLAND: THE ROUNDUP

The sun dangled dubiously down, casting shadows across a shadowy town on the edge of the Everglades. Another once-was boomtown peppering the South Florida landscape that nose dived into a cement swamp, and devoured by human gators slumming their way from day to day finally surrendering to the mosquitos and empty bank accounts. Thick summer air smelled of rotting Mexican food, junkies, hookers, and pimps. Marauding squads of gangstas prowled on foot, chattering and chugging from paper bagged bottles and cans, smoking weed and cigarettes. Souped up jalopies with heavy bass riffs cruised the avenue. Deep inland, where the neighborhood parents warned their kids about was booming with outcasts from a town that once was, but never would be again. The hospital closed years ago. The mall, mom and pop shops, chain fast food eateries boarded up as if the next hurricane came and went. At the intersection of despair and desperation there was a cannabis shop and a convenience store owned by an Asian family that'd been robbed on weekly intervals. There was an office building for startups that didn't, and a one-eyed dentist who rarely showed his face without his eye patch and Thompson .45 he'd taken as payment for a radiator grill of gold he adorned a pimp with. Next door was a two story medical center. On the second floor of the Golden Springs Medical Center are three offices. Two abandoned, one a dimly lit heavily littered corner suite. The X-ray view box shone a neon shadow on the debris.

Six men in military gear with automatic weapons, and two men in dark blue suits, sunglasses, and thin ties were gathered in one of the offices. The suits broke rank and stepped forward, standing in front of the man wearing a Stetson Skyline Cattleman Cowboy Hat. His legs stretched across the desk, and crossed at the ankles. The boots, handcrafted on both sides of the Rio Grande in Mercedes, Texas, and Leon, Mexico, embroidered in gold patterns pointed to the ceiling. He was leaning back with both hands on his belly, fingers laced together. The men in suits folded their arms across their chests and leaned in. One chubby and short the other, thin with a goatee and straw fedora. They waited a few beats and the fat man removed an ID wallet with a badge. "You're under arrest."

"That there's precious boys, git with the charges," the man in the cowboy hat smiled, revealing huge dice cube teeth.

"Murder, trafficking in stolen merchandise, treason, conspiracy against the USA, dozens of other details in the warrant. Yup you're the guy."

The man in the cowboy hat didn't applaud. "That there's not gonna sound legit fellas. Y'all got some rehearsin' to do before they show, ought say if they show."

"Shit, Willens, they were supposed to be here. We've gone over it for hours and searched the place ten times. I've been practicing this arrest schtick for what, three, four hours? They're not showing and I'm hungry."

Royal Willens stood, put his hands on his hips, and shook his head. "It's gettin' late Kurfew, and them rustlers he patched together. Uh uh. They're not gonna show. Uh uh they got tipped off, they's too smart for you Counselor."

"They may be too smart for all of us Roy."

"The Interpol filly, foxy li'l dock tramp, the jigaboo pilot-engineer you dumbasses couldn't lasso, and that ex-con plastic surgeon, Eddy. What did y'all find here?"

"We couldn't find shit, Roy." The puffy man loosened his necktie. "We've been here too long, and this dump smells like a greasy spoon diner, and I'm hungry."

"Have a durn donut fat man. What sorta dipshit doctor has a chop shop in this dump?"

“Edward Vincent, aka Eddy Vinnetti, formerly of The Federal Prison Camp, Pensacola Florida won’t have much use for the place other than a lay low, and Kurfew knows that Roy.”

“Dumb dago. Prolly got the eye-tallian mob in on this.”

“Unlikely Roy, Eddy is persona non grata with those boys. Something to do with an ex-wife. That’s all I’ve got, never met him.”

‘Dammit Larry this was supposed to be a head em off at the pass showdown.”

“I had reliable resources, solid intel, that this was where they were going to run after the frightener. Right here Roy.”

“Well they ain’t here.”

“Roy, be patient we’ll find them.”

"Iffen the real law don't find em first. Y'all best hope we do Counselor. I got the Ruskies on my back, and some simmerin' Chinamen."

"Roy, have I ever steered you wrong?"

"That'd be a big ole yessiree Bob. You said this shithole's where we round up those steers, and either brand em or gut em. Ya know I can git me some nice change for body parts, `specially kidneys this week. Too bad about the filly though, I right might be havin' some fun with the likes of her. After she shares some of that Interpol shit that is."

"We'll do better," the man with the goatee said. He would later reflect on the redneck money man's comment laced with the racial invectives, and go with the flow. "Yes Massah." In his best Steppin Fetchit voice.

Larry glanced at the thin man, "Have some respect big shot, you're still on Roy's shit list. "

Willens ignored the banter. “Good. We ought git on with things tomorrow when the smoke clears, and that there warnin’ I sent to the hotel kicks in. Ought have em right spooked. They’re gonna go for cover, and this here,” Roy gazed around the office, “ain’t where they’ll run. Ain’t that right Larrry?” He waved his hand in Larry’s direction. “I’m gonna git back to The Miss Demeanor, have me some supper, a massage, and outta this Tijuana wannabe dump.”

“I’ll ride you right over to the skiff boss,” the man with the straw fedora and goatee nodded. “There’s no room in the Rolls for the white boys in army drag, your crew. They’ll have to fend for themselves.”

“Hang on a sec, boy,” Royal Willens stood in the doorway, turned to Larry, and waited a beat.

“Larry, you’re a durn lawyer and this phony arrest may’ve been a good idea, but didn’t cut it. Gettin’ those crumbs believin’ y’all’re real feds. So far not even my dumb ole cousin Clem, who’s a collsarn retard, wouldn't buy it. Maybe we ought juss kill em."

"No Roy, I know what I'm fuckin' doing. This 'arrest' routine is not going to work, they won't merrily back off and confess. Kurfew's too smart for it. They didn't show cause they're in the know, and one step ahead of us. Shit, I'm a fuckin' professional. I know Kurfew and know what I'm doing."

"Do you Larry? Your shysterin' pert got yer ticket pulled. I hung with ya, cause you done right by me. Now alls ya gotta do is figure a way to wrap this mess in tin foil and deliver the goods."

"I got me some thinkin' to do Larry, and some folks to meet and greet in the mornin', so git yourself some chow and shuteye. I'll call you tomorrow."

"I can't wait Roy. What about him?" Larry pointed at Harold Spooky Pollack.

"Shit Larry get him some more fried chicken after he drops me off. I don't give a damn. Just make sure he don't disappear and washes that fine automobile case I need more chauffeurin'."

The man in the fedora had other plans. Driving the cowboy to and from the wharf, the schlep by sea to the yacht? No way Roy'd get a rerun of this episode. Harold Spooky Pollack calculated the odds of Roy's risk tolerance, being on US soil, and the possibility he might prefer having the subjects of this charade take place elsewhere, as in off the coast, and volunteering a personal touch by way of a gift to his new friend from Interpol.

14

BACK AT THE BEACHFRONT HOTEL
Thomas, Eddy and Chalk Head Out

The setting sun plastered the parking lot, baking gnats and thickened slushy air shimmering and making silhouettes above the parked cars with a quivering aura. It was the kind of heat that made shirts and skirts stick to skin like flypaper. The valet station facing west, wasn't spared the glare, and throbbed lazily over the maze of security gadgets. Guests and club members whispered in hushed chatter, spiteful bursts of complaints beneath the designer awning.

The valets parked the cars with the efficiency of insouciant smartphonery. Young tattooed men and women who'd had driven everything from Bentleys to limousines with the sort of precision learned from video games. The scent of weed hung heavy with an intoxicating slur.

A procession of polished paint, each car seemingly more expensive than the price of a liver transplant, drifted in an and out with the synchrony of a tuning orchestra whose conductor had Parkinson's Disease.

The valet parking attendant held the door of the Aston Martin for the driver. "Every light on your dashboard's flashing sir, and I couldn't get it to turn over at first," holding out his hand for a gratuity.

"What're friggin' nuts, kid? You want a tip for parking my car, and a lecture on auto maintenance. Piss off."

The car stalled. Chalk shook his head and blew out a whistling lungful, and in a syrupy deep voice said, "Thomas, he's on fumes, look at him, pathetic. Difficult to imagine he was an upright white boy once upon a time."

"Aw shit Chalk he's in a tough patch."

“Another tough patch? Life is a sum of all our choices. Edward defines poor choices thusly. He may inadvertently gum up this op.”

“I’ll take that under consideration.”

“I’ll do some recon, appreciate the gold coins you left in my vehicle. Um hm Thomas yes I do. It’s been too many years since you were in command. Do not go easy on him, and if the op fails be aware, Royal Willens does not take prisoners.”

“He does take hostages Chalk.”

“What about Mizz Interpol? I don’t trust her.”

“Either do I, but I’m sure she’s on to something, and whatever it is, it’s worth letting her run with it. Remember, she needs us. For what, I don’t know, but we’ll find out as things develop.”

“Thomas we go way back, the war, big time head up your ass practice, and the ex-wives draining you dry. You were broke until that funny business with Larry. You had it made, blew it, and now look at you, sucked into this shit. I know you’re having a time with the cutey, but she’s trouble son. Big trouble.”

An ancient red pickup truck chugged up behind Eddy’s ailing Aston Martin. It was coughing out smoke, and the driver’s door creaked open. A woman with a beehive hairdo and brown toothy smile stepped out.

“Bless your heart Chalk, y’all done here?”

“Hey Molly, right on time.” Chalk winked at Kurfew. “My ride’s arrived.”

***

Kurfew watched them drive off, inhaled, looked at the people awaiting and departing. They were a pampered slice of society sporting tans, chunks of jewelry dangling from necks, wrists, fingers, and ears. Designer threads and an oblivion pending on what's for dinner whispers. This was the high life of pre-season South Floridians. Folks who planted themselves year-round going through the motions of staying one step ahead of the next schmo on their way to the unpleasant process of aging miserably in a cycle of keeping up, breaking even, or losing it all. But what was it all? Everyone had their own set of circumstance, and meaning, drives, desires and defeats. No one seemed to be remotely off their inner galaxy despite the gunfire. Nobody notices anything, until it hits their orbit. Who knows, he thought.

As for Kurfew there was only the task, and the things he had to do along the way. From the islands to here, assembling the team to get where he was going, and where that was remained another piece of the same puzzle. Where the shapes had minds of their own. He awoke each day with a sense of urgency, maybe anxiety that wouldn't cease without some recognition that it was his energy reminding him there was only so much shit to give.

“Eddy, leave the car. I’ll drive,” Kurfew watched Eddy staring at the car, hands on his hips shaking his head imagining the fracas he’d unleash if he started to mix it up with the valet.

“T, I’ve had that friggin’ car for years.”

“Leave it Eddy, that heap’s about to die on you. We’ve got to have a talk with Chalk’s nephew.”

“Thought he was Roy’s bimmy?”

“Maybe not for long,” Kurfew’s car awaited. “Hop in Eddy, I’ll fill you in.

Engine humming, they slipped out of the hotel’s lot and onto A1A, the road unfurling like a half-truth. Evening lights of high end homes light traffic and palm fronds flickered in the mid-size rental car’s mirrors. Delray, Boynton, Lantana, the former Eau, a Four Seasons, walls of shuttered condos, small towns peppered the road, each with its own alibi. North of Sloan’s Curve, an adult theme park of generational wealth, celebrities, and tech wizard's second or third homes appear. Mizner Mediterranean mansions line the road's west side, each home a fortress against the have-nots and ordinary lives across the bridges. Towers of stone and slate slip behind gates; fountains gossip in concealed courtyards. Here the ocean is a private matter viewed through clerestory windows, or from terraces cloaked in Clematis, Wisteria and Honeysuckle.

Palm Beach waited unapologetically in the setting sun of summer.

Thomas and Eddy went over the details, global plans, and practical execution, until a silence pulling the car into the driveway of Harold Spooky Pollack's estate.

"You think he's here, Thomas?"

"Meredith phoned ahead, told him to expect us E."

"Are we gonna rough him up, or—"

"No, we're going to explain a few things, give him a choice. He's either going to burn Roy, or favor us with an invitation."

"You got a thing for the friggin' broad Thomas, watch yourself, she's trouble."

"She's another piece of the puzzle."

"Yeah, T, a nice piece of it."

15

IN OPEN WATER ROY GETS A VISIT

In the low light of the owner's quarters aboard the Miss Demeanor Royal Willens sat behind a desk carved from dark wood, and filled the room like a used car lot, a cup of something steaming in his hand. The room stretched out around him, mahogany and brass gleaming from the dawn’s light, weaving through the partially drawn curtains.

He leaned back in a zebra hide chair, legs stretched out, boots on the desk, and waited.

The yacht was equipped for a high-value art collection integrated into the design, with motion-sensitive frames and humidity controls. But there was no high art on board, not yet, just a gallery hungry for a taste of the old masters to be auctioned off.

The sound in the distance stirred Willens. It was a slow heavy pulse that grew louder with each groaning beat through the morning humidity, and ratcheting heat. He listened to each systolic murmur as it hovered above the helipad. The churning noise made the fluid in his cup shimmy, and his gut squeeze, reminding him the world still held things that could shred his empire if he wasn't on high alert. The yacht was not in international waters when his guests arrived. He knew in Florida international waters began beyond the Exclusive Economic Zone (EEZ), 200 nautical miles from the coast. This, Roy considered a buffer zone, and someone was always watching. Best to be safe if anything went bucking bronco. Sometimes the Coast Guard can be useful.

Three men of Asian descent stood in Roy's stateroom. Two wore high-end light colored suits, over t-shirts, sunglasses, the third man had on a darker suit and tie, and all three had what Roy would consider perfect hair.

“Gentlemen,” Roy stood “Welcome aboard,” and gave a slight bow.

The man with the tie stepped forward, removed his sunglasses and motioned the two to remain standing as he held out his hand to Willens.

“Mister Willens,” he sat in the center chair in front of the desk. Scanning the room he removed his sunglasses revealing red dyed eyebrows. He notched his chin at the two men who pulled back their jackets revealing their holstered guns.

“Howdy Yeung, I reckon y’all didn’t drop by with the Wu-Tang Clan for a social visit.”

“Hardly. Do you have the merchandise?”

“It seems, Yeung, we are at an impasse.”

“Impasse.” Yeung stood, “What is ‘impasse?’ We paid your people in good faith for—”

"Easy now fella, I do not have the durn paintings, the curator upped and disappeared."

"What is disappeared Mister Willens, the curator is in Shanghai, she is our guest. A very generous guest. She brought us many pieces of art. Nazi stolen art from the salt mines of Austria confiscated by the American government for bargaining with terrorists. She was part of that program, and came to us. We pay much better, and says YOU Willens have the means to bring us the rest. That was our arrangement. My people had the collection sold to private collectors around the world. They wait and nothing. You cheat us you die. We sink your big boat."

"She double crossed everyone didn't she?"

"She brought us four pieces, a Chagall, Cézanne, a Matisse, and a Pissarro. Four oceans surround the world my people hold as good faith payment for her asylum, and favor you with precious gems. Gems you spread like party favors with your mafias. Now where is our payment?"

Roy had to think fast. The gallery on board was empty.The curator gone, done sold out to the chinks? Triads, big trouble, fingers in everything and nobody's got em on their collsarn radar. The fuck. Kurfew and his crew been playin' fast to find both, and that shit lawyer Larry was figgerin' some angle to get square with whatever agency he could tie in with. Always figgered he was in with his Uncle Samuel to get square, but he ain't square with me.

"Hey Willis snap out of your trance. What you thinking? Some cowboy square dance from us? We are giving you three days to make good on our agreement. No more."

"I think Yeung, that I've got a leak in my team, a very fat leak and maybe—"

Roy's gun appeared quickly. A Colt .45, the kind that meant business. It was a piece from another time. All shine and intricate curves. Its engraving wasn't a scribble. It was a story that the metal would spit out with style. Gold and silver thread inlays wrapped around it. The grip wasn't dull plastic or worn wood, rather cool ivory, and aimed directly at Yeung's chest. "I don't jump at no threats son, either reset your threat clock or I'm gonna have Mr. Colt sing you a durn lead lullaby."

Yeung's men had their guns drawn and aimed at Willens. "Put them away, Willens is not going to shoot anyone. He knows if he does another will take my place, and another, and another. Do you understand that Willens? We are everywhere."

"We might be, but the you is gonna be hobnobbin' with your ancestors."

"That would be my honor Willens," Yeung, in one continuous motion swept his arm across the desk, a fraction of a second and turned the gun around, aimed it at Roy's head, cocked, and with a slight smirk set it down. "You are on notice Willens to respect our wishes. Three days," and put his hand in the side pocket of his jacket and removed a closed fist, hovered it over the gun, sprayed his fingers revealing his palm. There were three stones he let fall on the desk. “This is good faith that you do the right thing. An incentive to find and locate the collection.”

Willens stared at the stones.“Them there are right pretty Yeung, don’t see as many of these, as the other stones.”

“Jadeite, three million per carat. Three stones, three days, then the rest. And Willens we know you have been luring Kurfew to lead you to the curator and the collection, but what you do not know is the woman from Interpol is the curator’s sister.”

“What do you know about those rascals?”

“Everything, and nothing.”

“The hell, what’s that s’posed to mean?”

“Kurfew has no history other than a redacted dossier with the US Military, a medical practice, some marriages, what you call the straight shooting American success story that went bad.

He threw in with that go-between to sit on the goods with the curator. Either he's chasing the fortune, or the woman. We suspect he may have ties with some agency of the US but that is uncertain. I believe him to be a worthy adversary."

"You fellas do your homework."

"And you Mister Willens do not, despite the intelligence we provide. This ship, it is very impressive, equipped with the most advanced technology, armor, deep sea diving equipment, and fools to use it. Ha, Americans, too caught in social media, toys, and day to day hamster wheels. Your crew, idiots."

"I think we got off on the wrong foot Yeung. With that tidbit about the curator. It ain't Kurfew gonna lead me to the goodies, it's that sneaky li'l filly been up in my business. Nothin' like kin to hold a grudge."

"Stupid American sentiment is America's biggest weakness. Three days Willens."

Five minutes later Roy listened to the chopper's engine power up. He stared at the green stones and put the pistol away. Fuckin' dumb chink didn't even know tweren't loaded. Time to send an invite to pay me a visit on board, that dumb-ass Larry's phony arrest wasn't gonna do diddly squat, and that shyster probably knew it. He picked up his phone, punched in the numbers and made the arrangements thinking that fat fuck can manage it just fine.

16

AT THE SAME TIME BACK AT THE HOTEL

Kurfew awoke to see Meredith in the morning sun, sitting one leg over the other in a chair next to the bed. She wore a sleek black gown revealing enough leg to say hello, but not enough to say have a go. Her freshly coifed hair danced off tanned bare shoulders. She stopped rummaging through a matching bag she picked up at the hotel's gift shop after a few hours at the hotel's spa. Kurfew stared at her from the bed, and saw an understated elegance. He wondered if she might rejoin him, but considered last night's visit with Spooky, and the arrangement for a sit down with Roy Willens.

"You look radiantly intimidating Meredith, it's early what's the rush?"

“Thomas,” her voice was a mellifluous murmur. “Get dressed and wake up Edward. I want to know how it went with Spooky.”

“In which order?”

“Please, after you finish dressing. I don’t care to disturb the wanker before breakfast.”

“He’s hungover and harmless. And Spooky, we sweetened the pot, he’s with us all the way.”

Kurfew propped his head up on a pillow. “You do clean up well, c’mon back to bed I won’t muss your hair or ruffle your dress. Five minutes,” he pulled down the sheets.

“I was trying it on.” She stood letting her gown drop to the floor. “Five minutes, is that all?” She joined him.”

17

A LONG SHOWER FOR KURFEW

Thomas felt the water on his back and thought of what'd been, and how to play things out.

It had been nearly two years since the stash hidden within a canyon along the continental slope of the Cayman Trench, also known as the Bartlett Trough located between Jamaica and the tip of Cuba sat. The retrofitted WWII Type XXI U-boat where the stash of Nazi treasures was stored. The modified boat's hull retrofitted, and reinforced to withstand depths in excess its present four hundred feet. It had an anechoic coating and nestled in the canyon's volcanic rock formations and deep-water coral. Strategically located close enough, but not too far, from shipping lanes. The U-boat with its whispering electric motors, and thermocline layer made detection difficult.

The artwork was catalogued and stored in hermetically sealed, inert gas-filled containers, in a climate-controlled system with vibration-sensitive mountings. Retrieval of the pieces through specialized remotely operated vehicles (ROVs), launched through modified torpedo tubes was limited to pre-programmed tasks and challenges in unexpected situations. Divers wearing specialized gear, mixed-gas rebreathers, full face masks with integrated communications devices, and dry suits for thermal protection in cold water were the optimal choice. They would descend from the surface, retrieve the desired items through custom designed hatches on the sub, and return to the surface with lift bags inflated to bring the items gently to the surface where the boat's crew would be waiting. One man did it alone.

The trough, where the U-boat nested was known for its geological instability. Seismic activity was a constant. A significant tremor could do more than just rattle the U-boat's hull, it could trigger a submarine landslide, sending it tumbling into the abyss. Perhaps even burying the cargo under tons of seabed debris. Each dive wasn't just about the bends or oxygen toxicity, it was a gamble against forces grander and less predictable than any human plot. It wasn't about just retrieving art. It was snatching it from the jaw of potential catastrophe. Clock ticking and the earth itself threatening to reclaim its secrets, once and for all. Yeah, right he said to himself. It'd make a great fairy tale for kids and suckers.

Kurfew knew it. Four dives and the paintings he'd retrieved for Catherine, before her departure. Another dive could be fatal. In light of the recent seismic activity maybe this would be perfect timing to reveal an opportunity to Royal Willens who'd been itching for the spoils to sell off in exchange for precious gems. Kurfew's equipment was aboard the Miss Demeanor. Confiscated before his departure from the island. A foolproof gambit to let Roy walk himself to the gallows. Willens would take the bait, and do some fishing if the stakes were toppy, and Kurfew suspected they were entering the stratosphere.

“This might work,” he said out loud to himself in the mirror, drying off. There was something else nagging in the back of his mind, maybe it wasn’t just Roy. He stepped out of the bathroom, dressed, and watched Meredith adjusting her gown, “Let’s get things going.”

***

An hour later Meredith, followed by Kurfew emerged into the sitting area of the suite. Eddy was sipping coffee, Chalk sat across from him.

“I ordered room service while you two were comparing notes. Any revelations?” Eddy eyed the woman, “Lookin’ good there doll.”

She shot him a stare icy enough to chill his coffee a few degrees.

“Did you bring the equipment? The carry on items, you know we’ll be searched.” Kurfew scanned the Room Service cart.

Chalk held up his plate, fried eggs, very good Thomas, and for the lady?"

"Some fruit, and coffee, I'll help myself."

There was a soft knock at the door. "Thomas it's me, Larry, let me in."

"Someone smelled food, and guess who's coming to brunch? Must not've read the do not disturb sign. He can wait. Security's tight here, they may give him a shakedown." Kurfew stared at the door.

"Good, I'd prefer a body cavity search. The fool deserves it." Chalk shook his head. "I suggest we conceal whatever materiel from Larry, the semi-brilliant manipulator."

"That'd be a nice touch," Kurfew stood, arms across his chest. "I'm not letting him in, he sees us together? That'd foul things up. We'll meet him in the lobby."

“What’s with this friggin’ Larry the canary? A snitch, a double dealer, or another crumb workin’ his own angle?”

“He’s the one with the invitation and transportation. We were very convincing, getting Spooky to arrange it. Get well, or get drowned by Roy’s boys. We pay better.”

“I don’t know Thomas, the guy in Palm Beach didn’t seem hepped up about rolling over on Roy. And he sure wasn’t a dodgin’ bullets and mayhem kinda guy. I met guys like that in the slam. Cool as a stiff, then pussy out first sign of trouble. He did want out of whatever he had going with Willens, hangin’ over him, especially an unpaid debt.”

“My nephew’s a lot of things Edward, and being in a crossfire isn’t one of them. He’ll be ready for us if things go according to plan.”

“Chalk had a nice talk with him Eddy, so gather some reserve, you were only locked up for what six months? A white collar resort prison for tax evasion. C'mon, cut the hardcore shit. Get with the plan."

"We have a friggin' plan Thomas? Shit it was tax avoidance. The judge didn't care for the boob job I did on his wife."

"It's a play-it-as-it-lays maneuver Eddy, fast and loose. Meredith, Eddy, and me, we'll go with Larry."

"I don't recall meeting the friggin' guy."

"That'll be to our advantage. He knows enough about all of us to put in some screws, but he won't. Larry's a greedy shitbird, and that's how we'll play it. The three of us come off as needy and greedy, something Larry can relate to."

"Everyone on board?" Kurfew paced a few steps before pivoting and opening the door. Nothing.

"Feed the greed." Eddy nodded, smiled, and added, "Maybe butter him up with convict tales of the legendary go-between. He'd eat that shit up, huh?"

"Fine, if it fits. Larry's flattery operated, but he's dirty, This is a one-off for Larry, the feds cut him loose. He's in it for himself, and we can't let him know we're on to him. Not until I settle up with Romeo Roy Willens, so hang back Eddy."

"What about the woman Thomas?" Chalk didn't look at Meredith. "What's her part in this operation?"

"Meredith's Interpol connections came through with the dope on Larry when we were in Palm Beach. The whole scam beginning on Grand Cayman where I let Roy think he could play me as a mark. Put him exactly where I wanted him. She has her own score to settle, and that's between her and Roy. For now the need to know isn't hangin' heavy. Larry's waiting and we've got to go." Kurfew looked at Meredith, are we ready?"

“We’re ready. Spooky confirmed that we’re good to go. He made some arrangements with his uncle, Lieutenant Chalkman Davis, and me. Take a look Thomas,” her arm stiff, she held her phone out as if she caught and killed some contagious creature. “Here’s his text from late last night.” She swung her arm around showing the phone to Chalk.

Kurfew studied the interaction, raised an eyebrow, wondering, did she want his approval, or an acknowledgment. If so, why? “C’mon let’s get a move on.

18

TO THE MISS DEMEANOR

Beneath an angry sky the chopper approached the yacht. Bolts of lightning danced between clouds. The drizzle became dollops, the sky let loose a roar and downpour. The small craft bobbed up and down over waves pelted by liquid bullets. Sheets of rain hung over the sea like an opaque curtain creating a mist of uncertainty. An hour throbbed by, and through the watery wall the towering dark ship appeared, as if waiting beneath some magical umbrella. An immense beast of nautical craftsmanship, a dark island unfazed by chops and currents, immune from the elements.

"That friggin' thing looks abandoned." Eddy grumbled from the helm of the dwarf trawler. "No friggin' lights on, no welcome wagon."

“Shut the fuck up,” this might be a trap. “Radio Chalk, flying in’s going to be a bitch.”

One hand on the boat’s wheel the other on the throttle, Larry belched out, “Relax, we’ll be on board in a jiffy now that the storm’s passing.”

“What is a jiffy slim? Just get us on board.” Meredith joining them. She removed the rain slicker and matching broad rimmed hat.

“Take us around the boat Larry. Find the cargo hatch, maybe jimmy the retractable stairs. A passerelle, on the starboard side, maybe there’s a swim platform at the stern.”

Passerelle? Shit Thomas, a gangway or boarding plank, gotta get friggin’ fancy.”

“Easy you idiots, we’re not going to Gilligan’s Island, it’s a boat.” Larry raised his head, and puffed his chest with the uncertain certainty reserved for bullshitters crossed Kurfew’s mind, “and we’re invited, so there must be an easy entry point. I’ll find it.”

“I’m sure you will Larry. I’m sure you will.”

“What’s that supposed to mean Thomas?”

“It means if this is one of your side hustles, and you’re leading us into a trap, the kind nobody gets free of, maybe you’ve miscalculated, and that can be dangerous. My friend Eddy would gladly dispose of you. We have to trust you on this, and you know it. Am I right Larry?”

“You’re not wrong. Do you have a better idea Thomas?”

“Always.”

***

After boarding the Miss Demeanor, Kurfew, Meredith, Eddy, and Larry parted ways, and made their way through the dark corridors of the yacht before meeting on the deck. Kurfew insisted they avoid searching Willens private suite until they finished. No one questioned him fearing some hidden peril, a rattle snake, as in Roy himself, might be ready to chomp and spew a toxic venom.

Standing on the deck of the Miss Demeanor the search party looked at each other with a sense of wrongness. The ship was abandoned, no one on board, nothing disturbed, still seaworthy, still capable, yet it was an empty stage where a performance ended, leaving the lights, props and scenery behind. What Kurfew knew and the others discovered was not a derelict vessel rather a mystery without enough clues to be solved. There was a collective we've been duped and dread, combo platter of what the fuck fascination and sort of unease, that Royal Willens, and the yacht's crew had simply vanished into thin air. The Miss Demeanor was no ghost ship it was a ploy, and Kurfew watched the degrees of unease on Larry and Meredith's faces. Eddy shrugged, in a what the hell seen it all gesture. Nothing Kurfew said could prepare them for what's ahead, waiting in Willens private suite.

“Well, let’s head on over to the head honcho’s lair.” Kurfew lead the way.

“What’re you doing Thomas?” Larry’s face scrunched up in a a puzzled frown. “This better be good Thomas.”

19

IN ROY'S SUITE

In the overcast light of the owner's quarters aboard the Miss Demeanor a man of Asian descent sat behind the dark wood desk in what he considered a putrid imitation of elegance. The man's name was Yeung, Kenneth Yeung. Two men sat on a sofa across the room. They all wore dark suits, ties, and the red dye was gone from their eyebrows. Their hair was not perfect, but their aimed weapons were. Yeung heard the tap on the door, motioned one of the men to open it, and pressed the tips of his index fingers into his chin, forming a steeple with his hands.

The guests entered the room one by one, gazed around wearily, each frisked, and motioned to be seated in what Yeung considered a polite discomfort.

"Thomas Kurfew, it's about time. I am Kenneth Yeung and didn't think this would ever end." Yeung stood, held out his hand. "Good to see you my friend."

"Friend, that's a laugh, where's Roy and the crew, Kenny?" Kurfew didn't shake his hand. "This boat looks like the Mary Celeste."

"I gave him three days to produce, assumed he could not deliver. We watched him. He would not dare scuttle the boat, and do anything to avoid us. Triads are to be respected and feared. Willens was paid handsomely for what, nothing but lies. Our people report he was last seen boarding a private flight. He will find no solace anywhere. A man trying to disappear becomes a man living in fear. Ha. This fear will punish him until we dispose of him on our schedule."

"Hey Bruce Lee wannabe, you got some cohones. Whaddyou friggin' want from us?"

"Stand down Eddy, I've got this," Kurfew held a fist in the air.

“I want the coordinates, we have the ship, the resources, the equipment, the manpower and the time.”

Kurfew stood in front of the desk, hands at his sides, “You want the coordinates Yeung they’re yours.” Fingers curled, slightly bent knees, he turned his back to face Eddy, Meredith, and Larry, noting the two men across the room on the sofa had their guns drawn.

“How long have you had the location of the submarine Kurfew?”

“Before the day you walked past me at Romeo Roy’s bar when I was leaving. After giving Roy the convincer.”

“You are some sort of a grifter Kurfew, aren’t you?”

“I’m in the business of doing for others what they can’t do for themselves,” he paused for a beat. “For a fee that is. And with a little help from my friends we lured your people in. That's a bonus."

"We can pay more, much more."

"I doubt it Yeung, Uncle Sam's been very generous. Your organization tops the charts on everyone's shit list."

"So, you're with some three letter agency?"

"No, they call people like me when no one wants to stir any bureaucratic Q and A. Odd how I wondered what boy band you were with, but being at the right place at the right time was a clue I'd keep to myself and let double dealing Larry string me along. Find out how deep this art for gems scam went. The broad was a surprise, I rolled with her, the Interpol data may've been phony, but there was something else. Why go through the trouble for at best a wreck about to tumble into the deep? I retrieved a few items, that was enough, but the dirty doc and the gems, those are ours. She knew you boys had something on her. With Roy gone what else? Either way it was woven into part of Larry's maneuver."

"Did you call me a broad? I resent that." Meredith had a hand in her bag, fingers wrapped around a smartphone. In a flash it was pointed at Yeung. "It fires five rounds of .22 caliber bullets Yeung. Have your men drop their weapons, and step the fuck aside Kurfew."

"You wouldn't do that Ms. Gates. Nor would you knowing that your sister, Catherine, whom you've been trying to locate, is in China with four priceless works of art. We want the rest of the contents."

"Actually Yeung, it was five, the rest are Chinese relics the US was storing for trade negotiations with your country. Their value to the powers that be is negligible, and at my digression as long as Mr. Willens was dispensed with. And you wrapped that up Yeung." Kurfew turned to Meredith, "Don't do anything, not yet. There's a bounty on Yeung, and if he's got your sister maybe we can arrange something."

She took a deep breath and lowered her smartphone.

Larry's face sagged, "What about me?"

The roar of engines pierced the air. A plane spotted by Yeung's men passed across the ship's bow. There were three, maybe four boats surrounding the Miss Demeanor.

20

YEUNG'S DISSERTATION AND THE SCORE

Yeung's eyes narrowed. "What about you, Mr. Larry?" he said softly. "Your destiny is to be determined by a private tribunal in China. The United States has no use for you and your ways. You may suffer a case of accidental drowning before anyone sees your file."

"Why does the shit on board the sub mean anything to you Yeung?" Kurfew bowed his head and asked innocently.

"The Nazis made off with a fortune in cultural treasures from China. Many pieces remained missing, looted during the Nazi occupation. Exquisite Ming Dynasty porcelain, intricately carved Qing Dynasty jade, Buddhist statues and relics. Most important, are cultural relics from the Forbidden City, Imperial treasures, ceremonial objects, still unaccounted for, as was The

Portrait of a Young Man by Raphael, one of the most valuable missing artworks in the world. It could be worth over 100 million USD, maybe more. Isn't that right Doctor?"

The cabin door burst open. Chalk and his nephew automatic weapons in hand, entered the suite. "I heard that Mr. Yeung."

Yeung stiffened in the zebra hide chair. "Heard what?" Wondering if Roy's pistol was in reach, and decided a deal might be made. He motioned his henchmen to stay put. He saw Kurfew exchange knowing stares between the silver haired black man and the man in the fedora hat. They had him outgunned.

"Hello Chalk, I think we can wrap things up?" Kurfew looked into Yeung's eyes, "Do you think a mutually beneficial arrangement would avoid bloodshed, and an international flash point?"

Chalk's commanding voice captured the room. "I agree Thomas. I have the container you sent from Grand Cayman safely stored. Is it time to tell them?"

"Sure, why not? Portrait of a Young Man was taken by the Gestapo in World War II, and confiscated by the Chinese. Its whereabouts remained unknown until I saw Chinese labeling on a container on one of my deep sea dives. Artwork to buy out Catherine's share of the stash. Four pieces: a Chagall, Cézanne, a Matisse, and a Pissarro for the lady, and something special for my crew. Why the Chinese had it, shit who knows? But the US managed to get it back and put it with the rest of the goods "

"My people made a trade," Yeung said.

"The Raphael is the most important work of art, missing since the war. It's ours not yours Yeung, you can have the Chinese shit, and reunite Meredith with her sister, do that, and you'll never hear from us again. If you change your mind, this shit'll go far and wide. Some hard hittin' special op mercs can and will find you and yours, and their families anywhere.

This is a private deal Yeung, you and me. It ends here. You can always pin any shit on the cowboy. Think about it."

As Kurfew spoke he watched Yeung's rigid expression shift. A glimmer of amusement in his eyes, which widened slightly, a playful interest in wrapping things up. The Asian's lips curled into a slight smile, the corners lifting gently.

Yeung gave Kurfew a slight nod, lowered his eyelids, and raised them slowly, thinking maybe we could come to a mutually agreeable arrangement. Yes, he thought before speaking, this may benefit all and maintain harmony without bloodshed. A win-win. "I think we have a deal Kurfew. The items not only hold immense financial value they reflect deep historical connections to China's identity and heritage, making their retrieval crucial."

"What about my sister, Yeung? Is she your servant, or some sideshow dammit. I want her back?"

"She is in no jeopardy Madam Meredith. If you wish you are welcome to join her, and with the cooperation of your former employer we can ensure both of you safe passage."

"How about taking Larry for target practice?" Eddy volunteered. "I just met the guy and want to smack him."

Yeung glanced at Eddy, then Larry. "Would we have to feed him?"

"He's got enough dirt to fertilize a thousand acres." Kurfew thought a touch of humor would lift the cloud of tension buzzing in the air.

"We'll be on our way, Mr. Yeung," Chalk added. "In a day or two transport logistics will be complete. Our ride ashore is here. I take it this concludes our transaction."

"My men will ensure you reach the shore without interruption. I do have some questions for Mr. Larry though."

"If they involve electrodes to his testicles, I'd like some pictures to share with my sister Mr. Yeung."

"That can be arranged Madam," Yeung gave a slight bow.

21

THE HOTEL ROOM

The evening sunlight cast shadows across the faces of Thomas, Eddy, Meredith, Chalk, and his nephew Spooky. They were seated comfortably sipping beverages, no one spoke for fifteen-minutes.

Finally Thomas stood, leaned against a wall and folded his arms across his chest. "Chalk has the original, Eddy can dig into his favor bank from Club Fed and have his forger connection knock out ten copies of the Raphael. We'll float those to private collectors, and I'll present the original with Lieutenant Chalkman to the proper commissions. He might get a medal, I fulfilled my obligation to Uncle Sam, and we split the proceeds. By the time Yeung and his crew get to the trench the sub may not be there, lost to the depths. Meredith does whatever she has to do."

"That's gonna take friggin' time Thomas. My forger's got another few months. What about pocket change now?"

"Easy Eddy, show him Chalk." Kurfew notched his chin and shot Eddy a grin. "You'll like this."

The silver haired man put his hand in his jacket pocket, removed a fist, opened it slowly like a spider's legs releasing its prey, one dark finger at a time. In his palm, a plateau of stones and coins held out for inspection. They captured the evening sunlight, and emitted a glow sending shards of light illuminating his features, then the others casting shadows, and as those viewing would recall, an energy of their own.

"Are those for friggin' real, not some fugazi knockoff paste?" Eddy scratched his head. "They've gotta be worth a fortune."

"Yes, Edward. My nephew extracted the gold doubloons embedded in the Lucite counter at Romeo Roy's Bar, they were not fake."

Thomas added, “the gems and coins at Zillonius Crum’s office, his home, and in his dead body, there’s enough to go around to make all parties comfortable for a while. When things cool down. The rest in due time.”

Meredith stared at the gems, “I prefer the stones gentlemen. The Painite, Musgravite, Bixbite, and Red Beryl.” She used a tone reserved for corrupt cops, prison guards, and soon to be incommunicado bandits, who came across untraceable contraband on a perp, and smiled. It was a wicked smile, one that made men shiver.

It was as Kurfew would later recall, the sort of smile a thief wore after a heist, nervously wondering if they’d get away with it. Her eyes opened for a flash, before lowering her lids like a curtain, as if the show was over.

“That can’t be all you friggin’ want lady?” Eddy shot her an avaricious glance.

“It is Edward. I found my sister, you misogynist cad. The rest I’ll have no part of.”

“Enough bickering. I’m going to watch the sunset.” Kurfew pushed himself from the wall, slid the glass doors open, and stepped onto the veranda. Meredith joined him. “Thomas about my sister Catherine, did you ever love her?”

“I tried to, but business is business. I was none of hers.”

“And your business, rogue, boy-scout?”

“Meredith, if that is your real name let’s have a toast to China, your sister, parting ways, and what the future holds.”

***

From inside the suite Kurfew heard a symphony of ringtones. He had three, two in his pocket set to vibrate, and one in the suite. Eddy, Chalk, and Spooky looked at each other. Then Meredith, whose weaponized smartphone, purred like a herd of cats pissing on live ammo. Thomas stood in the center of the room, held up one finger in a hang on we'll do this all at once gesture. One, two, three fingers in the air. Kurfew first, "Hello."

"Howdy Doody y'all. I catch you rodeo clowns at a bad time?" Roy's voice crackled from the phone, the drone of the jet's engines audible in the background.

"Royal Willens, man on the move, very inventive having the phones ring at the same time." Kurfew spoke as if he was calming a nervous child before a magic show. He pictured Roy seated comfortably above the clouds.

"Y'all done did me right Tommy, them thar Chinamen were gonna do me some right fine misery. Word is you cut yourselves a sweet deal. Too bad y'all might not have the time to do much with what y'all think ya got away with."

“Is that so Roy?” Kurfew’s voice steady, as if he were reading a menu without any interest in ordering. “The name's Thomas. Anything else?”

“That there submarine and its goodies, I done forgot to mention the boobytraps that’re gonna send that bugger into the depths of Hades.”

Meredith, Eddy, Chalk, and nephew Spooky looked at each other, a tension hung between them for a few long moments.

“Y’all still there dummies?” Roy’s voice was peppered with coughs, and deep sputum producing wheezes.

“No, we went to friggin’ Disneyworld.” Eddy spit the words out loud enough for Roy to hear.

“Mr. Willens, Spooky said into his phone, “You remember me, the fedora hat, the island, and particularly the ride from Dr. Eddy’s inland office in my Rolls?”

“Yep, you’re the colored fella turned tail on me. Hope ya got that door handle fixed and that goopy shit cleaned up.”

“Mr. Willens,” Spooky continued, “take a look at yourself. You’ve been feeling weak, feverish, short of breath, ain’t that so?”

“What in tarnation are you sayin’ boy? Do you know who you’re talkin’ to?” Roy’s fingers tightened, squeezing the phone as if it was that sumbitch Spooky’s multi accented voice box.

“Why, have you forgotten?” Spooky’s voice had an edge sharp enough to slice through Lucite. “I’ve got a few words for you cowboy, all’d be punctuated with a nine iron, but considering your condition...”

“Lay it on me you goatee’d spearchucker.”

“Stop,” Kurfew interrupted and spoke to the cowboy the way physicians deliver a dire diagnosis. “Microencapsulated ricin at the right dose good buddy. The Chinese will write off the loss as an act of nature. We'll be off on our merry ways."

Spooky chimed in loudly, "It'll be a few days until your cracker ass is dead, Willens."

"Nobody fucks with me! I'm Royal Willens, so don't be so sure've your dumbass selves."

Chalk sat expressionless, wondering if perhaps his nephew had indeed grown some balls, and sipped his nonalcoholic beverage satisfied with Spooky's initiative.

Meredith raised her chin, lips tightened and the corner raised on one side of her face. It was a slight smile, a smirk. She stared at Kurfew, and lowered her chin before she.rolled her eyes. "I could use a bloody cigarette, there's a pack in my car. Thomas would you—

Kurfew's hand was on the suite's doorknob. He paused, notched his head to face Meredith. none of the men noticed the corners of his mouth raise briefly before leaving.

22

GROUND CONTROL WE HAVE A PROBLEM

Royal Willens sat in the plush confines of his private jet, engines humming a steady drone, feeling anything but serene. A cough rattled through his chest, sharp and constricting, a reminder of the ricin he'd been unknowingly absorbing through his skin. Maybe he thought it wasn't bull pucky, they got to him. Fatigue weighed heavily on him, stealing vitality as fast as the poison snaked through his veins.

He croaked out commands to the flight crew, "Git this bird on the ground, we ain't but an hour from Miami, and the Opa Locka airport." Hand gripping the armrest, "I done been poisoned, microencapsulated ricin," urgency in his voice. Which one of them did this? Thoughts fuzzy, the air felt thicker, oppressive, as if the cabin itself sensed his thoughts. "Get me some collsarn oxygen," he rasped, despair crept into his tone mixed with a heavy wave of vengeance. He eyed the overhead compartments, wondering what medical supplies might be stashed away. He rested his head against the cool window as he summoned whatever inner strength remained, trying to push back the dread of not getting the rodeo clowns who did this. Nobody fucks with Royal Willens.

As the jet vaulted through the sky he knew time might be slipping away. "Prep this bugger for an emergency landing, and round up my sumbitch docs outta Jackson Memorial. I got my boys on staff there, and make it snappy. There's a few million in it for you buckaroos when y'all get me fixed on up, I got their numbers on my phone." He glanced at the horizon where the executive airport loomed. Somewhere below, help'd be waiting. His people'd drop whatever they were doin,' and be there lickety-split. Each wheeze echoed memories of faces and places. Motives swirled in his the foggy head. All he could do was hold on, and let the rage keep him going. Searching feebly for answers, survival, and the dumbfuck's damnation'd be Romeo Roy's salvation.

Royal Willens staggered down the jet's steps. The clean air hit him like a slap, despite the fatigue. His specialists not more than a few miles away were arriving. Some already there, gathering on the tarmac a few yards away whispering among themselves mostly about the traffic, Roy's condition, and commiserating on how the patient may not be as bad off as Roy thought. Dermal ricin exposure wasn't as lethal as if he'd had ingested it, or had tears or open wounds in his skin. None were reported, but he was in need of care. The hospital room prepared, doctors, nurses, and techs on the ready.

Adrenaline coursed through Roy as he noticed a white sedan idling nearby. The driver's face, familiar, he was alone. Thomas Kurfew. The very man he'd tried to swindle for the coordinates of a hidden U-boat, a man with a keen sense of duty, a former soldier, mercenary, and surgeon. The low hum of dread settled in his gut as Kurfew leaned out of the window, a silenced Sig Sauer P229 pistol cradled in his lap.

“Thought you could outsmart everyone, didn’t you, Romeo?” Kurfew's voice was calm, cool, even, and matter-of-fact.

Willens took a hesitant step forward, weighing his options. Was it too late to negotiate or barter with a man intent on settling scores? Time was running out. The threat of getting timely treatment for ricin poisoning, and the gun, made Roy shit himself.

“Tommy, good buddy, we can work this out.”

Kurfew’s eyes narrowed and stared through him, the gun steady in his hand aimed at Roy’s chest. He fired twice. The silenced gunshots punctuated the tense air, muffled yet piercing. Two muted whispers of death. Nobody heard the shots. The driver unfazed, eased the car away from the scene blending into traffic as if the execution never occurred.

Thomas Kurfew avoided considering what's next.

www.ingramcontent.com/pod-product-compliance
Lightning Source LLC
LaVergne TN
LVHW090605110826
845146LV00001B/264

* 9 7 9 8 2 1 8 9 2 5 1 7 8 *